Gerald Rochelle *is a writer, editor and philosophical practitioner. His PhD was on the unreality of time. He has published books on time, general philosophy, ethics, grief, and the nature of self. As well as Forewords and Introductions to important reprints, he has published essays, reviews and bibliographies, edited a well-known Philosophical Journal and published twelve novels in various genres.*

Also by Gerald Rochelle

Cold Blood

APLtF

Goodbye: Grief from beginning to end

Goodbye II: Later reflections and a conclusion

Doing Philosophy

Behind Time

The life and philosophy of J.McT.E McTaggart 1866-1925

An Introduction to Philosophy in Schools Book I

Ethics Matter: An Introduction to Philosophy in Schools Book II

Also as Parvus Potentes

Piano People

BLOOD OF THE FLOCK

GERALD ROCHELLE

Not Equal Press

Not Equal Press

Copyright © Gerald Rochelle 2017

First published 2017

Not Equal Press

ISBN 9781535213660

For Pauline

Everything

'...and so the world runs away.'

Edward Senior

Prologue

Very soon the end of your life will be at hand: consider,
therefore, the state of your soul. Today a man is here;
tomorrow he is gone.
Thomas à Kempis, *A Meditation on Death*

Suddenly, on one dark day, and within the range of a single
thought, the air went still. Birds stopped singing, poorly
refurbished wind pumps failed to turn, un-replenished and
leaking water barrels were finally empty, and all were
encroached upon by a creeping, cloudy and noxious murk.
On this day—in an instant, in the spluttering flicker of a
guttered candle—all that had been modern became ancient,
all that had been hoped for became regretted, and all that was
evil became lost in the suffocating and impenetrable
blackness of what the past had now produced. On this day—
at the single toll of a hard pulled bell—the darkness that had
lain captured deep within the earth for millennia, and had
been released upon its grey and gloomy ground in the
shadowy form of Luit, finally overcame all that was. Now, in
this single moment, grey became black, shadows could not
form, and what had seemed endless was now over. On this
day the stench of Athala finally overran Atho, but any
witnesses could make no sense of it. As Atho's waters
curdled with the poisonous effluent that ran into its streets
through the conduit so its future began again. For Atho, in
time, when enough souls that could comprehend the world
would again walk its streets, when the cause of the sound
that spelled its doom was melted down and reformed into a
chalice and a mace for the new and never aging queen, it
would be the beginning of the new age—the age of platinum.

But for now, only the old ages had past—gold, silver, bronze and iridium had all fallen into a time gone by; and there would be a period of uncertainty and darkness until the new age was fully realised. The age had ended because a life had ended; the life that could only be killed at the hand of its own child, the seemingly endless life of Luit—half-brother of Graf, husband of Medean and lover of Sharka—had met that hand and succumbed to it.

1. Lezma

Luit stood beneath the massive trunk of a fallen tree. It sat heavily at an angle, perched on an embankment, still creaking with the strain of its own weight. He mumbled into his hands—a prayer, a request, an appeal to a redeeming force he only hoped existed.

'In Athala I have found immortal life but it is both a curse and a gift—it is my closest friend and my worst enemy. It gives me great power over others, for I have seen what they have not, but it also gives me a great foreboding for I know there is only one way my life can end. How can an immortal lose his life? It is ridiculous, but it is possible, for the reality of its loss is so much greater than the contradiction it presents. My accursed "immortality" can be ended at the hand of my own child—that is how it can be taken away. And what greater curse could there be; that the release from my inner suffering would be at my own child's hand? Please, God, if you exist, do not let it be so, not because I cannot bear the burden of everlastingness—I will gladly undertake that if it means my child will escape the misery of such an act—but because I could not bear the suffering of my own child living with the knowledge of such a terrible deed. Please, God, I appeal to you, if you have the power, do not let it be so, do not let me die at the hand of my own child. It would be a greater suffering than I could bear—yes, more even than the curse of immortality which hangs over me, more than the evil which it spawns within me, more than the terror I have of my own desires. Please, God, make me impotent, make me blind to the love of another, make me ignorant of my own desires, whatever must be done, but do not let it be so.'

He dropped his hands in despair—he knew there was no one listening, he knew there was no power great enough to act on such an appeal, but the utterance of it meant at least that he had heard himself.

Somewhere in Atho—a sweeter place—a little elfin creature darted between the trees—peach and almond, a streak of something translucent, the colour of flesh. It was a nymph, a sprite, a sliver of vitality brought into human living form. It was Lezma, Luit's impish servant.

The echoing voice of Luit boomed in her head.

'Lezma! Lezma! It is time to return. I am here again in your head. Come back to me! I have a need for you. Lezma!'

Yes, it was the voice of Luit, her master, calling her again as he had so many times before.

The lights in Lezma's darting blue eyes flashed brightly. She blinked and held the lids tight shut. She shimmered. She was an element—pure, perfect, untainted. For a moment she was in a dream—a moment of un-being; glittering out of time and place. When she opened her eyes and looked again the world had changed—she had been transported by his call to a different world. Had she run to him? Had she travelled for years to be again by his side? Could she possibly have made her way through the labyrinth of the conduit and not know of it? She could not tell—it had happened in an instant, it was too confusing for her to piece together.

She widened her nostrils and inhaled. This place she now found herself in had a different but familiar scent. The sweet fragrance of Atho had been replaced with the heavy musky tang of her master, Luit—she was back in Athala, breathing in its stinking air, ready again to be in his presence. A thrill ran through her body at the thought of again being in his company, of running to his commands, of doing his bidding. The stinking air of Athala—she could not take enough of it into her lungs.

She sucked it in and held her breath. She swallowed the scent of her lord's domain—feeling it running down her throat and entering her visceral self. It was like feeling him inside her. She tightened with a moment of fear—the pleasure of her return was mixed with a sense of

4

apprehension. Now, she must face him, the one who had dispatched her to Atho in the first place. A shiver of anxiety went through her. For a moment she could not tell why, then she realised she had been slow to respond. She tapped her feet on the ground apprehensively. She knew he had called her back earlier, and she had not wanted to return—she knew she had disobeyed him. She could remember that much. Sometimes, when she was in Atho, she forgot her errand and followed her own will. Sometimes, when he called, she pretended not to hear him—just for a few more minutes of delightful independence, maybe an hour, maybe more. She gasped for breath and looked impatiently from side to side, desperate to see him again, eager to place herself at his mercy.

He had sent her to Atho to collect another to join the flock. He had built his herd like this, choosing individuals he thought would benefit from the opportunity for immortality, those who could join him in his endless and burdensome everlastingness. And they came eagerly although not all of them were suitable. Some could not receive the seed—they bled too much and their bodies rejected what he fed back into them. But they were not wasted—he used them up, as food amongst the others and as parts for his rotting body. Lezma was their escort. Sometimes she played with them a little on the journey—just a game, a little pleasure, perhaps some kissing or running away from them and leaving them in the dark until they cried. But this time he had summoned her before she could even collect the one chosen. She pushed out her bottom jaw and pursed her lips. This time it was Luit's fault that she had returned empty handed. If she was late this time, it was his fault not hers. She stamped her foot petulantly on the ground. Yes, this time she would tell him so as well!

Lezma knew the labyrinth well. He had taught it to her carefully—drilled her in its twists and turns—and she could fly through it as though she had wings. She turned this way and that without a thought; she ducked her head beneath

5

its low arching roofs, or squeezed herself between its confining rocky slits without ever seeing anything in its impenetrable darkness. There were places where she had to wade, and one place where she had to cast herself in bodily and swim beneath a hanging mass of black rock. Then, as always, suddenly, as if the journey had not happened at all, she would find herself looking up at his ragged face, on her knees before him, panting, squinting her eyes up in the murky light, waiting for his command in the rain of Athala.

She wiped the water from her legs. As she ran her hands down her naked body, she realised that this time she had swum further, waded deeper, and struggled longer through the wet mire that bordered the final pond. Yes, the final pond had almost engulfed her! And there had been more water to struggle through than ever. Now, as she wiped it off her smooth skin, she saw that there were streaks of black in it, and it smelled—powerful, noxious, overpowering. Yes, it all smelled! And her legs ached so much!

She ran to a patch of long wet grass on a raised knoll and plunged herself down into it. She rolled, like a joyous foal, sweeping her arms and legs across it, pushing her face between the wet green blades—cleansing herself of the black smears, freshening herself, renewing herself for her audience with Luit.

He was close by. His nearness turned the stench into the sweetest scent. The thought of the sunlit, sweet-smelling pastures of Atho made her shiver with perverse disgust now she was back again in the acrid atmosphere of Athala. How strange, she thought, that the good could seem so bad and the bad so good.

She darted between some wet trees. Droplets of rain lit up her skin. She saw a group of shambling inhabitants shuffling wearily through the rain. She wondered if they would survive the drenching; in Athala it sometimes rained so heavily, and for so long, that those caught in the open drowned.

6

The heavy clouds pressed down on her frail body—
she felt their weight. She shivered and bit her lips. She could
still taste him on them. She pressed the backs of her hands
together and squeezed them between the tops of her thighs.

She stared through the sopping air at the sad,
shuffling creatures. Each day was worse for them—less light
broke through the clouds, and ever heavier, more insistent
and unforgiving rain beat down onto their aching heads. As
the murky daylight faded, they gathered together for
safety—lost souls milling in the confused tribes that were
Luit's flock. Cast into darkness and overrun by shadowy
forests, these ragged inhabitants stalked their dim world,
travelling from one spluttering beacon to the next in the
misplaced hope that, while parted from their lord, the feeble
source of light may offer a replacement sense of refuge. And,
unable to rest, they plodded on wearily, stumbling from cave
to makeshift hovel in the hope of finding a safe haven—a
place to shelter from the rain until the dawning of the next
dreadful day and the search for the next meagre source of
light.

There was a sudden flash of lightning, a rumbling
crash of thunder. Lezma crouched down in fear at the base of
a rain-sodden oak. Some of the flock fell to their knees. They
clasped their hands together and turned their eyes upwards.
They scanned the murky clouds, looking vainly for a miracle
to cure them of their never ending misery—a fate they had
chosen but which now pressed on them only with dark
foreboding. Their fate was eternity, to till their unproductive
earth with split and suppurating hands, to bear the
everlasting suffering of an eternal future, to trudge rain
soaked and shivering until the end of time.

Some of them saw her and cried out.

'Help us! Help us!'

She giggled, amused by their sudden outburst.

'Help who?' she shouted back mockingly.

'*Us*! Help *us*!'

'Who are you?'

7

'We are members of Luit's flock, and we are afraid for our future.'

'Help yourselves then! It is *your* future!'

She sniggered at their confusion and threw herself back down on the wet grass.

Another flash preceded a heavy roll of thunder. Lezma pulled her shoulders up and bit her lips. A blue talon of lightning reached down from the black clouds. It penetrated a man on his knees—a half naked wretch, already begging for release from this place to which he had mistakenly been brought. The thunderbolt rent him in two; like an unfulfilled androgen, his body split down the centre. Each charred side fell heavily to the wet ground. Steam from his boiled organs rose up in misty wisps into the darkness.

Lezma jumped to her feet.

The cracking thunder subsided. There was an eerie silence—a moment of stillness. The others lifted the limp charred remains of the man and carried them away into the darkness. They would hide him from Luit and use him themselves. He would not be saved from eternity yet. He would provide for their nourishment before his task on this earth was completed.

Lezma suddenly became aware again of her thumbs against her naked cunt. She had not noticed how welcome they had become. She squeezed them against the flesh for a moment—pinching it with her nails, filling herself with ripples of joy. Then, like a goodbye kiss—filled with longing and disappointment—reluctantly she pulled them away.

She knelt and pressed the palms of her hands together. She touched her thumbs against her lips. She mimicked a prayer. She wiped the rain from her face and giggled. He was close! Yes, very close! She must not let him think she was hiding.

Lezma called to him from the darkness of the trees.

'Master! Master! I am here, Master!'

The air was clearer in Atho, there her throat was less congested, but here in Athala, her cry was shallow and broken.

She coughed.

'Master! I am here!'

She had to force the air from her lungs to make it sound.

'Master! Master!'

Her wavering hail skimmed between the slivers of mist that curdled brown between the heavy trees. A waft of the dead man's burning organs suddenly came into her nostrils. She cocked her head to one side and listened.

She called again.

'Master! Master!'

She knew he was nearby—stalking her perhaps, watching her, checking up on her. She brushed her hands back through her wet hair, rehearsing a story to excuse herself should he challenge how slow she had been to return.

She rushed towards where she thought he might be.

'Master! Call back to me. I cannot see you. I am not used to Athala's darkness yet. And we are so far away from a beacon.'

There was a movement. It was him.

He turned. He recognised her voice. Syrupy tears ran in the cracks on his face. They broke into gluey rivulets as he smiled with pleasure at her homecoming.

Rain dribbled from the tangled ends of Luit's long, grey hair. He looked from behind the wet curtain of matted web-like strands like an ancient spider. He stared out as if from another place—a soul buried deep in a distant world behind his vacuous yellow eyes.

There was a moment's lull in the rain. A glint of sun trickled between the grey, shifting mass of clouds. It brought a sudden burst of warmth, a fleeting respite before the next downpour.

Luit turned his patchwork face into the light. He stretched his neck painfully. Eternity had taken its toll. His body was worm-ridden, salvaged and recovered by his own hand from his victims. He had sewn himself together from

9

flesh he had stripped from those whose meat he had eaten. And he suffered under the weight of his knowledge of it all—his own evil and his unending destiny savaged him with their continual presence.

He breathed in the heavy air. He licked his tongue out, catching a refreshing spot of rain, which heralded the next downpour. But it brought no refreshment, no novelty— there was no such thing in this oppressive everlastingness, which was his life.

Lezma's eyes lit up as she saw him. She was filled with excitement—overflowing with the joy of anticipation. She ran forward as if to a lover's arms. Boiling with excitement, she ignored the unmoving girl that lay at Luit's feet; his victim's fate was irrelevant to her—the girl's blood-soaked body no more worthy of notice than the tangled tree roots that wove like snakes beneath the sodden trees. Lezma had long since become accustomed to the sight of suffering at Luit's hands—indeed her heart quickened at the thought of it. She fell on the ground before him and looked up at him, panting like a puppy, filled with pleasure at being back with him again.

2. Mistia

Lezma knelt at Luit's feet. He laid his hands on her head as if giving absolution to a sin worn supplicant. She shivered at his touch. She saw the girl in the corner of her eye—she could not hide her distraction from him.

'Are you jealous, little Lezma? Of this other one? Of this one you pretend not to see?'

Lezma looked down at the girl's face as it stared blankly towards the leaden sky. She recognised her—it was one of her playmates. She tried to think of her name and found she had forgotten it. She felt a sense of hollowness in her stomach at the gap in her memory. A shiver of confusion came over her.

The girl's dark hair was long and reached to her small pert breasts; Lezma thought them about the same size as her own. Her arms were twisted together, like vines clinging to each other in a desperate attempt to reach the light. Her legs were wide apart, her naked flesh exposed, the crack at its centre parted, its swollen edges glistening with a translucent slick of moisture. Deep teeth marks were cut into her cheek, the back of her jaw and into her neck. Blood had run from all her wounds and had flowed in rivulets into a main stream that had gathered in the depression of her collarbone. It had brimmed over from there and streamed down her chest. It had spread across her breasts and dripped from her small hard nipples. It had run down her stomach then, stemmed by the rise of her hips it had followed the curve of her waist and finally dripped onto the ground.

Lezma stroked the girl's hair. It was wet with rain and greasy with sweat; some blood stained it at the ends as though the strands themselves had bled.

'Why should I be jealous, master? I know I am your favourite.'

'Tell me the truth, little Lezma. The truth, I say!'

He coughed with the effort of raising his voice.

'We all envy those you grace with your favours, lord.

11

How lucky they are. But you know my happiness derives from yours. How could it be otherwise? If she gave you happiness then I am rewarded. Jealous? How could I be jealous of your joy, my lord? I revel in it.'

'You please me so much, little Lezma. And yes, she was indeed succulent, my little elf. She did indeed give me joy. Her blood was hot and eager to run. It streamed into my mouth. I fed on it as she moaned. I drank it as she begged me to bite her again. She trembled in my hands, hoping that I would cover her with bites, hoping that I would rip her flesh and consume it while she lived through the pleasure of it. Does that make you jealous, my little imp?'

Lezma tightened her eyes.

'Lord, I am happy just to be close to you.'

'And see her crack, my darling Lezma. It is like yours—naked, precise, perfect. Think of my finger running along it. Picture its moist edges opening at my touch. Can you imagine how I have used it, my little fawn? Would you like me to use yours in the same way? The truth now!'

He coughed again.

Lezma bit her lips. Tears welled up in her eyes. Her heart was racing. Her veins throbbed in her throat. She could not speak. She felt her head pulsating. She wanted to stamp her foot. She wanted to shout at him, to tell him she hated him. She wanted to pinch him and pull at his ragged rotting flesh. She wanted to rage at him. She wanted to spit at him and kick out at him angrily.

'No, my lord, I am not jealous,' she said throwing her head back and closing her eyes for a moment. 'You could use me like that if it pleases you, master. You could say her name as you did it to me, master. Your joy is my only pleasure. I would not begrudge another the pleasure of your attention if that is what you chose.'

'I am not sure I believe you, my dearest Lezma. You are squeezing your eyelids tightly together, as though you are holding in something you want to say or do. I do hope you are not trying to deceive me, my little elf. Is that possible?'

'That would be impossible, my lord. Impossible!'

Lezma ran her fingers down between the tops of her thighs. She felt the heat of her own flesh against their trembling tips. She looked again at the girl. Suddenly she remembered her name—Mistia. Lezma had been swimming with her often. How could she have forgotten her name? They had both played with the boys. Yes, it only seemed a day ago since they had been together, naked, with the others. She had kissed her. Yes, she had kissed her and punched out at her in fun. They were a good match as playmates. Mistia's lips were full and succulent. Lezma remembered how they had felt against her own—silky, delicate, eager and wide. They had both dived into the water and splashed the boys. They had chased each other—diving and swimming in circles around the channel markers. When she caught her, Lezma had held Mistia's head, dragged herself up onto her shoulders and pushed her under the water. Mistia had cried out as she had burst again to the surface in an explosion of water, bubbles and spray. Mistia, of course! Those beautiful, full lips, those taut limbs, those screams of delight. She had kissed Lezma back so keenly—they had pressed their mouths together, they had sealed them so tightly, they had breathed each other's air and consumed each other's passion. Lezma again tasted Mistia's tongue in her mouth—she sensed again its sweetness and warmth. She remembered how she had sucked at it, how she had drawn it into her mouth. She had felt its tip probing around her own tongue. She had felt it pushing along the insides of her cheeks. She had sucked saliva from it. It had tasted so sweet, so delicious. Mistia! Even her name was sweet. Mistia, Mistia—she could not get it out of her head.'

Luit's voice broke her reverie.

'You may enjoy her for a moment if you wish, my dear Lezma. She is not dead. But only a kiss—no more!'

Lezma swallowed in a gulp.

She bent her face down to Mistia's. She smelled her

blood, her sweat; the two perfumes mixed together into a fragrant and heady aroma.

Lezma felt spit forming in her mouth. It ran along the edges of her tongue and onto its tip. The hinges of her jaws ached with anticipation. Her mouth dropped open. Spit dribbled over her bottom lip. It ran onto her chin. She licked it back. It was cold and frothy. She could not contain her excitement.

She pressed her lips against Mistia's. They were plump and full. Lezma opened her mouth but Mistia's lips did not move. Lezma drew back and gently licked along them. Again she sealed her own lips against them. She pushed her tongue into Mistia's mouth—it was cool, still wet with spit. Lezma licked Mistia's tongue. It was moist and refreshing. It moved under her caress—limp but still succulent. Lezma pushed her own tongue in further. Its tip reached the back of Mistia's throat. She poked it as far as she could. She tasted Mistia's breath—acrid and delightful.

Lezma ran her hand down across Mistia's blood-soaked breasts—they were small and firm. She circled them with the palms of her hands then pinched the hard nipples tightly between her thumbs and forefingers. Lezma let her hands slip in the blood as she rubbed them around each breast. Mistia's nipples poked between Lezma's outstretched fingers. Lezma pushed her hand down further, across the shallow of Mistia's smooth stomach. She stretched out her fingertips until they touched the front of Mistia's crack.

Lezma waited there—filled with the delight of anticipation, frozen and boiling in a fevered confusion. Her heart beat rapidly; she widened her eyes thinking it had stopped. Her head was pounding. She drew her tongue out of Mistia's mouth. She licked the inside of Mistia's lips then ran them down her chin and throat, across her bloody breasts and onto the mound which led to the front of Mistia's cunt. Lezma pulled her finger along the delectable crack. The soft glistening flesh opened at her touch. She poked her finger in. It slipped in easily. Lezma pushed her mouth closer until her

14

lips were against the yielding edges of Mistia's slit. She probed her tongue against it, into it, along it. She licked the base of her own finger. She tasted Mistia's moisture—heady, sweet, aromatic. She licked deeper. She pressed her finger in more. Mistia's moisture ran onto the palm of her hand. She slurped at Mistia's cunt. She fed on it. She drank her fluid. She drenched herself with it. She shook her head from side to side, she rubbed her face against Mistia's flesh, she covered herself with Mistia's delicious moisture.

Lezma knew she had disobeyed him—she had taken more than a kiss. She lifted her bottom. Her taut buttocks rose up in an enticing, eager curve. Luit raised his hand. Lezma sensed the movement. She brought her bottom up higher. Her head was giddy with anticipation. She delved Mistia's cunt with her tongue. She rubbed her cheeks and her nose against the swollen flesh. She waited for Luit's admonishing hand. She held her breath. She listened to her pounding heart.

One sharp blow—one sudden, penetrating smack. Lezma reared back—filled with the joy of pain, her master's touch, his control, his anger. It penetrated to the very core of her being. Straight away, she dropped onto her back, her legs apart. She gasped loudly. Her face was wet—smeared with blood, her own spit and the moisture from Mistia's cunt. She licked her lips. Her eyes were wide and bright.

A spot of rain fell on her breast. It was cool, isolated and sudden. Then another fell, this time on her throat. She felt as if the drops were piercing her skin. She wanted Luit to bend to her and bite her. She wanted his teeth piercing her skin. Another drop touched her forehead, another caressed her other breast. Then more fell as the next downpour began again. She opened her legs as wide as she could as, in seconds, the rain turned into a deluge.

Luit reached down to her. She took his hand keenly. He brought her to her feet, squatted down and lifted her onto his lap

'There have been losses, my little imp. Perhaps there

15

is a breach or maybe something is blocking the conduit?'

'It is a mystery, lord.'

'But, Lezma, you are the escort!'

'It is not my fault, master. I take them to the last low roof near the entrance on the Atho side and leave them. They can make their own way from there. Master, I have found my own little tunnel! Aren't you proud of me? I love squeezing through it. It comes out on a mossy bank near...'

She realised she should not have said anything about her deceit.'

'...but I look out for them on the other side, master! I am like a hawk!'

'And you have not noticed that some you have taken have not returned?'

'No, lord. I count them when I leave them and I count them again when they come back. One...two...three...four...I am a real little abacus. Look how I count, sire!'

She spun around giddily, shouting out numbers at random.

'It is puzzling you did not notice anything on your last journey. Still, if you had you would have told me, I know.'

'Oh, yes, I would, lord,' she said falling sideways dizzily. 'Though I don't like to trouble you with detail. You have so much to think about.'

'Come with me. Wipe your face.'

Lezma looked down at Mistia. A bubble of spit bloomed up between her lips.

'Leave her, my imp. I will come back for her later. I think I might let her recover and train her to take on some of your errands. She would be a good companion for you, don't you think? She could help you with your counting. She could make sure there were no mistakes.'

Lezma squeezed her eyelids tightly together. She jumped in front of him and led him away. Suddenly, she turned and ran back.

'I must just do some counting, lord. I will catch you up!'

Luit smiled as well as his cracked face would allow.

Lezma dropped down at Mistia's side. She looked towards Luit. He was not looking back.

The bubble of spit on Mistia's lips was slowly expanding as a long slow breath escaped her lungs.

Lezma pursed her lips and crinkled up her eyelids.

'You will not do my errands, nor check my counting; I will make sure of that.'

She poked her forefinger and index finger of her right hand into Mistia's nostrils. The bubble expanded more as Mistia's airway was blocked.

'My master will not find favour in his heart for you, my playmate. How sad it will be when he comes back to you. How sad that you will no longer be able to respond to him when he bends to you for a kiss.'

Lezma drove her fingers deeply into Mistia's nostrils, pressing them hard and holding them there until the bubble burst and no new one was formed.

Mistia's mouth dropped wide open.

Lezma twisted her fingers and stretched Mistia's nostrils.

'And now you look like a pig!'

She pulled her fingers from Mistia's nostrils, jumped to her feet and ran after Luit.

'Master, see how I catch you up like a flash of light!'

3. Fah

Lezma danced around Luit as he walked. She felt elated. She looked at her arms, her legs, and her naked body—inspecting them as if they were not hers. Her skin glinted in a brief flash of sunshine that shone between the black clouds. She dipped playfully, whooping and hooting like an owl.

'Hoo-hoo-hoo-hoo! Hoo-hoo-hoo-hoo! Look, master. I am a wise owl! Hoo-hoo-hoo-hoo!'

She coughed and cleared the congestion the thick air of Athala brought with it. She dropped to her knees and kissed the ground—it was wet and exuded a powerful musty scent. She jumped up and wiped the soil from her bloody lips. She swung around in circles, her arms outstretched, her eyes turned upwards to the black and blue-patched sky. Another sudden burst of sunlight dazzled her. She clasped her hands over her eyes and ran on blindly until she tripped and fell. She rolled along beside him and pinched playfully at his ankles.

'Are you happy for me, master? Do I delight you?' she gasped breathlessly. 'Are you pleased with your little owl?'

He blinked his heavy eyes slowly.

She rolled forward in a ball, jumped up, somersaulted then pounced forward and nipped the greying skin of his wrists between her finger and thumb. She dropped down again and rolled in the wet grass—she bathed in it. The wetness from the rain covered her pale peachy skin like cool honey. She twisted and shook herself. Wetness sprayed from her in a shower. It burst in clouds that shone in the beams of light that broke in coloured rainbows from the hanging branches of the age-old trees.

'Master. Master. Do I bring you joy? Master, do I?'

She ran to catch up. She turned a cartwheel. She scampered ahead, swung around and ran backwards on her heels.

'Look, sire. I have eyes in the back of my head. Now,

I am a beast. See me growl.'

She widened her legs and hung her arms down like a bear. She giggled and laughed as she wiped filaments of red wet hair from her beaming face.

'Oh, Lezma, you breathe light into my dark world. What would eternity be without you? How could it be bearable in your absence? Here, swing on my hand. Let me feel the weight of your body. Let me feel your life, your vitality.'

His words thrilled her. She ran to him and clung to his hand. His skin was rough and clammy. She squeezed it tight. Touching him delighted her. She jumped and bounced on it.

'I want to hang from you like an ornament, lord. I want to be a trinket, a necklace, something to shine at your throat. Oh, lord, let me adorn you, let me sparkle for you, master, let me glitter for you.'

He bit onto his cracked lips. He swept her up in his arms, turned her back against him and clutched his arms around her waist.

'Now, my little imp, you must be serious. You fill me with too much joy. Here, look at the flock. See how they cower and shiver in the cold and rain. Have you seen them that way before?'

She wriggled from his grip and ran towards the shambling group of souls huddled beneath the trees. She danced around them and pulled at their hands as she circled them.

'They are simply your flock, master. They are the ones you have selected to receive eternity. How can they be troubled when they have your company forever?'

Luit approached.

'Look, my sweet. When I press between them they shy away. They have a new fear. They do not fear only me; they fear the absence of my guardianship. My promise to them is under threat—I can sense it. They suspect they cannot be sure of continuing life—that terrible gift I have

19

assured them. Or perhaps it is the fear of the gift itself?'

'Surely, master, they are only fearful of being in your presence, excited by it, overwhelmed by being so close.'

'No, it is not that. I told you there have been disappearances. Ones I have sent to bring back relatives or chosen ones have never returned; no matter how well you count, my little imp, fewer come back than are sent.'

'I always do my duty don't I master?'

'Yes, yes, my imp, of course, but even so, the ones you told me you have brought back have not been there when I have gone to find them.'

'Then they must be hiding, or lost in the rain. Perhaps they have been split in two by thunderbolts and have hopped away?'

'Put your hand on your heart, little imp, and tell me you have never found any missing when you have returned.'

'Master, I can say with all my honour, that I have never brought back fewer than I have taken. You know I am your truly honest little imp, master. Look how I clasp my heart!'

'I have had some of the groups counted, Lezma. One sorry band has lost eleven. Eleven! I can only think that something has corrupted the conduit—it has been breached or blocked. But you would have noticed it wouldn't you? I am confused. How was your last journey back, my little imp? Tell me!'

Lezma could hardly think—she was too excited, she did not want to bother any more about her duties. She tried to picture her last journey in her mind.

'I cannot remember, master. There was a lot of water. Yes, more than normal. And there was tightness, I think. I recall having to squeeze. But I am small. I wriggled through. Look how I wriggle!'

She twisted herself around him. She clawed her hands beneath his armpits and wrapped her knees around his legs.

'You were too keen to return to me. Perhaps you did

20

not notice in your haste. You always come at my first call, my sweetness. You are so obedient. But we cannot afford these losses. If the flock are too few they will weaken. If they are weak they will lose the will to face eternity. And sometimes even you are not enough for me, Lezma. I also need their company to face my fate.'

Lezma began rubbing her naked crack against his leg. The rough material of his breeches tugged at the soft flesh. A thrilling heat reached up inside her. Her eyes widened and her mouth dried.

'But you always have me, master. Tell me how I can be enough for you?'

'Lezma! Look, there is the sister of one who has been taken—one of the eleven that have been counted as lost. Lezma, my child, tell me, do you know her name?'

He pushed Lezma away. The thrilling heat inside her subsided. She pouted and looked down at her feet. She knew the woman but was keener to show him she was annoyed. She looked away and stamped her foot.

'Lezma!'

She turned abruptly, her eyes tightened, her lips pursed.

'It is Fah, master. She came here as a child. She has spent much time serving you in Atho. She has made many journeys to encourage others to come here. Look how she has aged during her absences. Her face is lined and ugly. How we all suffer if we are away from you for too long. Feel my skin, master. Feel its smoothness. Feel how silky it is for you. Even though I am away from you often I do not age—it is because I am so overjoyed when I find myself at your side again!'

He ran his cracked hand across Lezma's smooth forehead. Her eyes brightened. She clutched him eagerly.

He pushed her back again.

'Has she done her duty, my little one?'

Lezma scowled.

'Yes, master. She has worked hard for you. She has

gathered many. I have counted them myself! See, they still cling closely to her. They think she is their mother. She is like a goose to her chicks.'

Lezma dropped to the ground and rolled in the grass. She flung her legs apart. A fresh heat penetrated her as she exposed her cunt. She looked up at Luit. She imagined him on his knees between her legs, licking her, lapping at her slit.

Luit ignored her and turned to Fah.

'Fah, come to me.'

The woman, wearing only a tattered skirt, approached nervously. She brought her shaking hands together and knelt before him.

'I have wronged you, my lord?'

'I do not know. Have you?'

The ones around her clutched at Fah's ragged clothing; their only comfort was the security they found from being close to her. They detected the fear of her uncertainty, their sense of security faltered and they could think of nothing but to cling closer.

'Fah, my little imp tells me you have served me well.'

'I have, lord. Yes, yes. Reward me with your punishment. I am eager for it. Suffering at your hand is my only pleasure.'

Lezma pushed forward. She pinched Fah on the cheek. Fah closed her eyes and sighed with sudden delight.

'Look, master. She needs some pain. Give her some pain, master. Let me watch you make her suffer. She wants to suffer, master. Make her suffer. Master! Master!'

Luit grabbed Lezma's red hair and tugged her back. She scowled.

'Where is your brother, Fah? He came here with you. Can you point him out?'

'No, he has been taken, sire. They all talk about it. When we journeyed with your escort to Atho under your instructions, he was with me. He was holding my hand near the entrance on the Atho side, then suddenly he was gone.

Although some say you called him back to Athala for some special reason, when I returned I could not find him. Is it possible that you called him, master, and that he did not come to your summons? Is that possible, sire? Could he refuse your order? No, surely that is unthinkable. He must have displeased you in some way. Have you expelled him from our world? Did my brother wrong you, sire? Yes, that must be it. And am I to be punished for his wrongdoing? Have you selected me to suffer for his misdemeanour, sire?'

'I sent him with you and my little imp to bring back your children.'

'And I have one here, lord. Look, it is Fahlene. The other, a boy has been lost as well as my brother. We entered the conduit but he wandered off and became lost in the darkness.

Her eyes filled with tears.

Luit sniffed at the air.

'Do you need pain?'

'Yes, master, always.'

Will it make your life of eternity more bearable?'

'If it is part of my service to you, master, yes.'

Lezma tugged insistently at Luit's arm.

'Test her, master! Test her! How can her child have been lost in the conduit when I counted him? She is lying, master. I would not have let him wander off. I would have tied him to a string and tugged him behind me. Master, she is lying to you! Test her, master! Let us find the truth, then you will know how well I serve you.'

Luit pushed Lezma away. She scowled but could not stop herself hopping with excitement.

'Fah, do you feel the need to serve me with your pain? Do you feel it deeply within you?'

'Yes, lord.'

'Does that need course in your blood? Do you feel it beating in the flesh of your crack? Does your flesh swell with the thought of it? Do you feel the trickle of moisture along its slit as you picture the hurt in your mind?'

'Yes, I do master. I do.'

'Show me your mark.'

Fah lifted her ragged skirt. She pushed her naked hips forward. She pointed to the smooth skin where her left hip dished inwards to her flat stomach. Two weeping sores trickled with blood.

'Has it been many years?'

'Yes, lord. I was only a girl. Yet still my blood runs. You came to me the first day I was here. My mother was already yours. Do you not remember, sire? I dream of it every night.'

'Take this knife. Let me see its blade slice into your flesh. Let me see your blood run afresh. Look, my little imp will hold out her hands. It can drain into the cup she makes with her fingers. See, she does it straight away. Oh, my dearest little fawn, she is so excitable.'

Fah did not hesitate. She did not even consider where to place the blade. She took it from him and drew it against the closest part of her body—her left breast. She dug the point of the blade into the dark pink areola. Her nipple hardened as the tip of the blade pressed into her skin. It throbbed as the blood seeped out. She did not flinch—she was serving her master, enduring pain for his pleasure, suffering because of his will, sacrificing herself for his eternity. There was nothing more in her world she wanted to do. She dug deeper. The blood ran more freely. It seeped along the blade, its silver metal reflecting through it like moonlight, making the oozing fluid appear translucent.

Luit drew a long heavy breath. The scent of the blood filled his nostrils. He closed his eyes and inhaled it. Its thick scent—musky and bitter—stuck to the hairs at the entrance to his nose. He licked his grey tongue up and tasted it. He breathed in again.

Lezma pressed herself against him. She pulled her arm around his hips and ran her hand across his buttocks. She ran her fingers between them.

He pushed her away. She tightened her lips and

24

scowled. She dropped her head. She knew better than to let him see her annoyance. She looked up under her eyebrows and pouted. He would push her away once too often, she thought. One day, when he tried to quell her eagerness, she would fight back—particularly now she knew he was thinking of training another to do her job. Yes, one day, she would kick him in the shins, or poke him hard with her finger, or bite at his hand—that would show him.

Lezma shrugged petulantly. She walked away, then suddenly turned and clung to him again. She grabbed his finger and sucked at it. She licked around it. She spread her spit along it, and then sucked it back into her pert lipped mouth. She swallowed it down. She belched.

'Suck her sores, master. Suck her sores.'

Luit smiled.

'Cup your hands beneath her nipple, my little one. I want to watch her blood running into your little bowl. Do that for me, my imp.'

Fah sighed. She pressed the blade deeper. She twisted it. The white layer of fat was exposed beneath the pink surface of her skin. Blood ran over its edge and stained the whiteness with crimson stripes. Fah took a long breath. She closed her eyes. She paused, and then slashed the blade downwards. It tore through her flesh in a long straight line. It cut her skin open from the edge of her erect nipple to the base of her breast. The firmness of her breast eased as the wound opened and its meaty mass was released. Blood gushed from the gaping cut. She lifted her chin, tightened her jaws and, as if pinioning herself to infinity, held the blade where it was.

Lezma knelt excitedly in front of Fah. She could see Fah's pain; she could see how it was being held in. Lezma felt the stifling sensation of unreleased anguish. The flow of blood would carry Fah's agony and her pent up suffering and Lezma wanted to taste it.

Lezma brought her hands together. She mumbled a mock prayer then opened them out to form a cup. She pressed her fingertips against Fah's chest and held the cup beneath the wound in Fah's breast. The blood ran freely into her waiting hands.

She looked up at Luit as her bowl filled.

'Now?'

'Yes, my little imp. Refresh yourself. It is your reward for being so faithful, for doing my bidding, for always telling me the truth.'

Lezma squirmed her knees together. Shivers of excitement ran through her. They started in her thighs—tensioned by kneeling—and spread upwards into her buttocks. The soft flesh of her cunt was squeezed together tightly—the crack at its front could not be seen. The strain absorbed the stress from her thighs. She tightened her buttocks and squeezed hard. She felt the pressure in her anus and along her crack, but the aching sensation only increased. It spread up her stomach, across into her hips and higher until she felt it in her small pert breasts. Her nipples, already hard, throbbed with the increased pressure; it was as though she was being pulled on strings attached to them. As she moved her arms they tightened more. Her head was giddy. The veins in her neck and in her temples pounded. Her mouth was dry. She panted heavily.

Lezma dipped her face into the bowl made by her hands. Her nose touched the pool of blood first. She smelled it, inhaled its delightful, heavy aroma. She dropped her head forward a little more. The crimson fluid touched her lips. She tasted it—thick, metallic, salty. She opened her mouth to it and let the tip of her tongue touch its viscous surface. She gasped and held her breath with the delicious shock of it. She dropped her tongue further into it. She lapped once and stopped—for the moment, she could stand no more. She waited, hoping that the pressure of excitement would ease; that she would be released from her enforced and unwanted inaction. She lapped again, and again she was shocked and stultified. She waited once more. She screwed her face up with frustration. The pressure eased again. She sucked. At

26

last, the red liquor bubbled into her mouth. It gurgled and frothed over her tongue—thick, glutinous, sticky. She sucked in more. It filled her mouth full. She felt it run on the insides of her bulging cheeks. She shivered as the overwhelming sensation of delight took hold of her. The blood started to coagulate in globs on her tongue. She rolled the glutinous balls against the roof of her mouth—gummy, viscous, and adherent. She trembled all over.

She dropped her face fully into the pool of blood. She felt it sticking to the balls of her eyes. She looked into the redness. She stared through the living blood. She was infused with it. She blinked—the gluey strands stuck her eyelids together. Her eyelashes were thickened by it. She breathed in and sucked it down; she could not tell whether it was entering her stomach or her lungs. She felt herself drowning in it. She welcomed the suffocation—the overwhelming flood of it.

Luit placed his rough-skinned hand on Lezma's shoulder.

'For me, my little one. Do not be too greedy. It is for me that the blood flows. It is for me that the pain is being endured.'

Lezma looked up. Her face was covered in blood. It ran from the corners of her eyes in sticky crimson tears. She opened her mouth in a frustrated grin. Her white teeth were stained red and strands of gummy redness dripped from their ends. Reddened spit frothed over her open lips.

Still on her knees, she turned to him. She felt a waft of cool air against her crack as her parted thighs momentarily exposed it. Blood ran down her chin and dripped onto her aching breasts. It stretched out in thick strands from her hard extended nipples and gathered in the creases formed at the tops of her thighs. She felt its sticky moisture working its way into her crack. She squirmed on it, and made its journey to her eager flesh easier.

She offered up her hands to Luit.

He tipped his head forward and drank from her bowl.

27

Blood ran down her arms and dripped from her elbows. She lifted her cup higher for him and the red elixir ran under her armpits and down the delightful curve of her slender waist. Her eyes, now washed clean, stared out white against the red of her face. She held her hands in place until he had finished—until his thirst was satisfied, until he had drunk his fill from her offering.

The anxious flock pressed around him. They pushed at each other, eager to get to the front, eager to see more clearly. A wave of excitement spread amongst them. A wizened and grey old man bit into a woman's arm. She turned on him and smacked his face with her sinewy hand. He bared his teeth—a drip of her blood fell from the broken edge of one of his upper canines. He stared at her—uncertain what to do. She held her hand up, ready to strike again. A young girl pulled at the woman's torn skirt. The woman looked down to the girl. The old man saw she was distracted and, his uncertainty galvanised into a sudden outburst of rage, he launched himself at her. She fell back in fear as he drove his teeth deeply into her neck. She screeched in fear, pain and the confusion of relief.

Annoyed by this disruption to his feast, Luit turned to them angrily. He opened his mouth and hissed. The old man froze, his teeth still buried in the thin flesh of the woman's bleeding neck. Luit tightened his eyes and hissed again. The man allowed his jaws to slacken. Blood bubbled from the woman's neck. It ran down the old man's chin and soaked into his dirty white shirt. It looked as though his heart had been ripped from his chest.

Luit held the back of his hand beneath the old man's chin. The woman's warm blood streamed down across it. It ran down the backs of Luit's claw-like fingers and dripped from their horny ends.

The others pressed closely around him; incensed by fear, the suddenness of activity, and the scent of flowing blood. Some dropped low and turned their faces up towards the dripping blood. One woman, naked and scarred by misuse and lack of care, lay on her back and opened her mouth wide. The others jostled and pushed. Some exposed their teeth, or hissed and spat. Some growled or grunted. All were anxious to feed from the hand of their master—to taste their share of the blood and to feel the safety that came with his closeness.

He allowed them all to be nourished, lifting his fingers away only when they were licked clean. One by one, his blood-soaked acolytes lay back against each other—for the moment satisfied, their anxieties stalled, their fears put into abeyance. But Luit knew this was a temporary pause—the worries that constituted their deep anxiety would again soon run up to the surface. He had to act if he was to save them from the fear of losses from their number, from the terror that threatened the certainty of his domain, and from the weakening effect of depletion.

Luit walked in the rain. Lezma gambolled around him. Occasionally, he stopped and watched his herd as they stood huddled in small groups beneath the shelter of dripping branches. They clutched each other, shivering, moaning, and squeezing their eyes tightly together for fear of what they might think. The infection of terror had spread amongst them quickly and it had become distilled into a pure form of fear, one that knows no direction or cause, one that burns away inside the soul like a festering abscess. His flock was weakening; his kingdom's strength was seeping from the open sores of their insecurity. He closed his eyes. If there was a breach in the conduit, he must repair it, if it was blocked, he must free it, if it was flooded, he must drain it. By whatever means, he must release the flock's terror, cauterise their wounds and restore their calm. The supply of new blood must not be stemmed. Without it the flock would only weaken and wither. He saw a few crouching at the edge of the river that flowed into the conduit; they drank water from their cupped hands. In that one act he saw the desperation of the situation that faced him—the flock quenching their thirst with water! Even Luit did not know what would happen if they dribbled their spit back into the river. It would surely be poisoned, and that poison would run through the conduit, but what that would mean he could not imagine.

4. Medean

It had been many years since Luit had found a way through the conduit from Atho. He had suspected since a boy that there was something to find behind the massive scree of fractured rocks that fell from a chasm between two folding grassy meadows. He traced to its source, the river that brought water through irrigation ditches and channels to the green pastures of Atho. Eventually he found the leaching drain that sprang from deep beneath the shattered rocks and beneath that an opening large enough to enter. Knowing where the water came from became his obsession.

He prepared a flaming torch and held it inside but it was immediately extinguished—the air would not sustain it. No effort he made to provide light worked and in the end he accepted its impossibility. He spent years penetrating the darkness behind the entrance. There, in the blackness, he followed tortuous tunnels, crawled on his belly beneath heavy rock roofs and, fighting desperately against his own fears of water, swam ice-cold subterranean rivers and lakes as he made his way further inside. But for all his efforts the labyrinthine cavern would not yield up its secret. Many times, exhausted and hungry he had re-traced his hard-won steps down countless blind alleys only to find nothing but disappointment and despair. Thinking that only insanity would save him from the hopelessness of his quest, and on the brink of dejection, one day, pushing a boulder aside in anger, he finally emerged into another world.

It was empty then, unnamed and unpopulated but, as he took his first breath of its air, he knew it offered something that was beyond the confines of a normal life. He felt a surge of heat in his body, a glistening, a refreshment that transcended anything he had ever known—in that single breath he felt the infusion of eternity. He realised that he was breathing in something that was part of a different form of existence—something not confined by the mortal. Here, in the air of this new place—sodden by incessant rain,

31

burdened down with darkness—lay the very seed of life. Here, in this shadowy wetness was a hitherto hidden spell, some magic of the gods, something of what was thought of only as a myth, a real remnant of the fabled iridium age. Here was immortality. He felt it in his veins after that first breath, and from that moment on he knew he need not die.

He slept at the exit for a week and did not return to Atho for a year. Many, including his half-brother Graf, thought he had died.

First he built a beacon so that if he wandered from the exit of the conduit, he could find his way back. In the wetness he found it difficult to light and hard to keep the flames burning and he had to attend to it constantly. Looking for dry sticks beneath stones he found a black scorpion with yellow spots on its pinchers. He crushed it and it emitted a lime green fluid that glowed in the dark. He found more and rubbed their bodies on the beacon stand so that he could always find it again if it went out.

Even though it seemed impossible that anyone else could find their way through the conduit, within its dark labyrinth, he added false trails and dead ends so that penetration of it was truly impossible without his aid. When he felt it was completely secure he named the place "Athala".

He walked the rain sodden forests meditating. He knew that while here, his life would be endless but the penalty of eternal loneliness soon started to hang heavily upon him. He decided he would populate Athala and so bestow this new flock of souls with the gift of everlasting life; they would act as companions as he lived on into eternity. With the idea came a fresh excitement—the excitement of their blood, a sensation he had never before had was now running through his mind—the yearning for blood. When he was ready, he returned to Atho and took some back to Athala who had become worn down with illness and suffering or who saw the new world he offered as the answer to their mortal fear of death. These first few were recognised by the others as pilgrims; monuments, paintings and images were erected in tribute to their pioneering bravery and they soon received sacred status.

Luit had always been the master of Atho but, after his discovery of the new world beyond the conduit, he took on the additional role of messenger and preacher. For a while he evangelised in the church, announcing the good news of his discovery and calling for any to come forward who were willing to enter the new world. To begin with they flocked in scores, fighting with each other for the right to submit to the endlessness of this promised new life.

He soon found that in Athala, like him, some did not die. He did not know why only some survived but found that he could nourish himself with the blood of those that didn't and so satisfy this new hunger that now ran deep within him. But his immortality was incomplete; he had been too long in Atho for the air of Athala to preserve his body. As time went on, he found it began to degenerate—parts of it rotting or peeling away, parts becoming continuously infected or septic. To remedy this he made use of the ones that died by stripping their flesh and with it repairing his own.

One day, he found Lezma—naked, red haired, slight and beautiful. She was shouting and turning cartwheels beneath a massive wet tree. She did not age, and she remained his favourite, and his special messenger, and he taught only her how to find the way through the conduit. In giving her this honour he also bestowed on her his trust. Lezma revelled in his presence and guarded his special companionship jealously.

As time went on, Luit found it more difficult to make the journey back to Atho—an enhanced terror of water caused him to suffer too much anxiety and when he did return it took him many days to recover. He sent Lezma by herself a couple of times but she could not convince any to return with her, though she said she tried very hard. He decided to send others back under her escort to convince relatives to return with them—their bloodline made it more likely that they would survive and it was probable that they would be more easily convinced of the efficacy of the migration to Athala from those that were close by kinship. He instructed Lezma to act as their guide through the conduit and to conduct them back with the new ones they brought. He found that it was possible to summon her by calling into the Athala entrance to the conduit. She would somehow hear his voice and soon return with her charges. He sensed a special power that flowed when he called her. He did not know whether it was contact with this power, the thought of coming again into his presence, or the journey through the dark bewildering labyrinth, but when she returned she was always confused. Over the last few years, she had become more difficult to summon and sometimes he was more troubled than amused by her increasing petulance.

As the flock increased and Luit now stayed all of his time in Athala he used Lezma not only as his errant messenger but also as his confidant. As the cloying air of Athala permeated his body it affected his spirit. His appetite for the blood of others increased and mostly could not be satisfied—he was continually thirsty for it and suffered a constant gnawing in his innards that was only temporarily assuaged by feeding on fresh blood. And the further price of his immortality—the degeneration of his own body—caused him increasing suffering. His use of the body parts of those of the flock who did not survive was a painful process that he undertook only out of obligation to his own endlessness. He sat for days sometimes, perhaps on a fallen tree in the forest, or beneath a spluttering beacon, tearing off skin from a dead body, cutting it carefully to match some of his own which had decayed or rotted away, and sewing it in place.

Once, in the early years, after he had been preaching all morning from the pulpit in the church in Atho, he sat on the gentle hillside above the town. It was warm and he was uplifted by the idea of an eternity of infinite delight. A group of women sat together picking chaff from winnowed corn. A slender beauty in their midst stood out from the others. Her dark tangled hair hung loosely on her shoulders. Her peachy skin was covered in a satiny bloom of powdery dust from the corn. It picked up light from the sun and reflected a shimmering sheen around her like a cloud of gold. Her eyes were dark and wide. She sat up on her knees. A thin vest barely covered her rounded breasts. The way she had tucked up her skirt behind her feet had pulled the waistband down and exposed the shallow curve of her slender waist. Her full lips revealed bright white teeth when she laughed. She stood out like a single blooming flower in a barren desert.

A group of men stopped and chatted to the women. Suddenly there was a flurry of activity as the beautiful dark-haired woman was dragged to the ground. The other women stood back, holding each other fearfully and shouting as their friend was pinned to the corn strewn earth.

The men tore off her skirt first. She wore nothing beneath it. She twisted her naked hips as she fought against them, but they held her ankles fast and she could not escape.

Luit watched as they yanked her skirt up over her head. She screamed at them and snapped her teeth, but it made no difference. The other women saw Luit and called to him, beseeching him, pleading for his help, but he did not respond and remained quiet, watchful, and inquisitive.

The men took turns with the woman. Each knelt between her legs, dropped his breeches and penetrated her eagerly. Some drove themselves into her cunt; some lifted her hips and pushed into her anus. As they pulled out and made way for the next, Luit saw the gleam of their semen dripping from her fleshy cunt or running from the dark centre of her dilated anus. As he watched, he picked at his broken fingernails with his teeth. Occasionally he spat bits onto the ground, but he never took his eyes off the woman.

She snapped at each of the men as they took her, showing neither sign of pleasure nor indication of relinquishing her resistance. Suddenly, she managed to twist one of her hands free. She reached across and grabbed the wet penis that had just been pulled from her cunt. The man cried out in surprise and fear. He lessened his grip and in so doing allowed the woman to free her other hand. She sat up and gripped his testicles tightly in her fist. His eyes widened in horror as she reared forward and sank her teeth deeply into the shaft of his penis. Blood spurted all over her face. She did not let go. The man shrieked. She tightened her grip on his testicles, sucked out the flowing blood then, without a second thought brought her beautiful white teeth together with a sickening snap.

As she pulled back—the man's amputated penis still dangling from her mouth—she yanked her hand back and ripped his testicles away from his body. She held them up like a prize—twitching sinewy red and white flesh dripping with blood. She spat out his penis, dropped her head back and took the raw bloody testicles into her wide hungry mouth.

She chewed on them for only a second before swallowing them both. She did not pause. She threw herself forward, buried her face against the man's blood-soaked groin and sucked the bubbling crimson flow of blood that issued in beating frothing spurts from his severed veins.

The other men fell on her and tried to pull her away but her grip was so tight they could not separate her from her screaming quarry.

Luit got up, spat a large piece of one of his nails onto the ground and walked slowly down the hillside.

The men drew back as he approached.

He stood above the woman and the screeching man. The woman was covered in blood; dust from the corn stuck to it in grey-yellow patches. She twisted and squirmed still in the throes of her violent seizure. Luit bent and ran his fingers through her blood-soaked hair. She sensed him immediately—even as she drowned in the passionate tide of pleasure that overwhelmed her, she sensed his touch. She shuddered and went still.

She turned to him, her face red with blood and with fleshy tissue hanging from her gaping mouth. He looked into her eyes. He had known since he had first seen her from the hillside that he wanted her for his own.

She was called Medean, and she went with him without hesitation. She never inquired of his history, never asked about his rotting body, his hunger for blood, of the pensive weight that seemed to bear down on him like a thundercloud. She listened to no rumours or tales—she simply loved him. She did not question him calling out Graf's name as, in the throes of his passion, he drove his venous shaft between the open fleshy folds of her cunt. She did not question his desire to make her wait on her hands and knees as sometimes in the dead of night he strode naked around the walls of Atho bellowing defiance to his half-brother. She did not deny him his obvious pleasure and taste for the delights of punishment as he dragged her by the hair into the town square and caned her upturned buttocks as the old women spat on her and threw clods of mud at her agonised body.

He stayed with her for many weeks; his passion now turned to an uninhibited delight to dominate her and feel her subjugation to his will. Most days he took her to the city square and stripped her naked before he knelt between her legs and penetrated her. He favoured her anus but she showed him that she wanted his semen in her cunt as well. They slept together alongside the altar in the church and often inhabitants of the city would come and look at them both while they slept, some keeping vigil over them throughout the night, others simply content to sleep in their proximity. A rumour spread that Luit would stay in Atho and that Medean would become his queen.

As time passed, Luit became increasingly anxious for the flock's well being—at this time they were still forming and needed his constant reassurance. He left Medean while he journeyed back to Athala. When the inhabitants of Atho came and found Medean sleeping alone they blamed her for their loss of Luit and, lighting candles on the altar and reciting incantations, they cursed her and all her progeny.

37

They stoned her as she ran cowering into a small chapel built in a crypt beneath the foundations of the church where an old witch looked after her.

When Luit returned he found Medean pregnant. He took her from the chapel and had the old witch walled in; they found her powdered bones many years later when the church was reconstructed.

During his absence, the inhabitants' hatred for Medean had consolidated. Every night from then, as Luit and Medean slept, the townsfolk gathered around the church and chanted curses. Sometimes Luit ran out to them, threatening to tear their limbs from their bodies but always, by the time he got outside, they had scuttled away and found hiding places in alleys, dark doorways or behind grain stores.

He could find no midwife to help him with the birth and he delivered the child himself. He thought he could pass his power onto it, and that it could become his heir, so he decided to take Medean and the child back to Athala. As they made their way to the conduit, women followed them, dodging behind trees and sometimes throwing stones or clods of earth. When they arrived at the entrance of the conduit they found Lezma sitting on a rock, naked, pressing a leaf to her nose and sniffing it. She jumped down as soon as she saw Luit and ran in circles around him.

'Do you want my help?' she sang. 'I can carry the baby. I am a wonderful servant, master. Let me. Let me. Let me.'

As they made their way through the conduit, Lezma ran ahead with the child in her slender arms.

Lezma knew every part of the tunnels. Sometimes she ran on ahead into the darkness and was lost to earshot, then as they made their way forward slowly she would suddenly surprise them as she jumped out around an unseen corner, laughing and dancing in excited circles.

Medean found the journey hard and terrifying—the oppressive blackness and echoing noise steadily increased her anxiety and fear. She stumbled many times and struck her head twice where the rocky roof dropped lower without warning. But she did not complain or draw attention to her distress and Luit assumed that she was happy and excited to be travelling to the new world.

When they arrived in Athala, they found the flock nervous and unhappy. One of them, sent to tend a distant beacon, had been lost. They had listened to him calling out for several nights but his calls had gradually got fainter until, finally, they stopped. On the first night the lost soul had tried to follow the sounds of his companions' cries but had gone the wrong way. Some said that he had disappeared in a great mire, some that he had been consumed alive by a woman with serpents in her nostrils that guarded the outer kingdom beyond the light of the beacons. Stories about a wilderness beyond the range of the beacons soon spread, as did the fear of an eternity of loneliness and isolation cut off from the company of the flock.

Medean, beautiful as she was, looked haggard and dirty after the journey through the conduit. As the anxious flock gathered around the entrance and saw Medean, now holding the child in her arms, their pent up anxieties turned immediately to hatred and rejection.

Luit did not speak. He watched the angry flock, confused by fear and tormented by their nervousness, as they milled around blinded by rage and hatred. And he saw the frightened face of Medean, taken from her home in Atho and brought into this foreign land through the terrifying blackness of the conduit. He saw etched in the dirt and bruises on her face that her suffering was not for her desire to live forever, but only to be with the one she loved.

That night Luit slept with Medean and the child beneath the first beacon he had built. The flock sat around them and throughout the night Luit listened to them fidgeting and mumbling as they lay sleeplessly on the wet ground.

In the morning, a woman known as "Treasure" was pushed forward from the flock. She was one of the first handful Luit had brought to Atho—one of the celebrated sacred pilgrims.

'Sire, I beg to speak.'

Luit nodded his acknowledgement of her seniority amongst the flock.

'You have brought a curse back with you, sire. I can say it in no other way.'

He reared forward on his haunches and hissed. She shrank back and screwed up her sunken eyelids.

She breathed deeply and forced herself to continue. Her hands were shaking as she spoke.

'Sire, it is true. A curse is with us. It has been spoken of for as long as we know. It says that your death will spring from your own loins. Sire, if this is your child, it will spell your end, and with it, sire—I beg you, forgive me, sire, but I must speak—it will spell our end as well.'

He reared forward angrily.

'How can this be so? You know I cannot die!'

'I do not know, sire. And I can hardly speak the words. I know only what is said. The child is a curse to you, and its mother brings the curse as she brings the child.'

Luit bent forward and put his crinkled face in front of Treasure's. He spat at her; his saliva ran down the lines in her cheeks. She was shaking but did not dare move.

Luit looked at Medean, her dark eyes wide with fear, the child wrapped in dirty rags held close to her naked breast. As if for distraction from the conflict, or in response to her maternal responsibility, she presented her nipple to its open mouth. It turned away its clear blue eyes and stared— as if peering out into eternity.

A man ran forward. His face was reddened, bursting with fear that he was unable to hold back. Drawing confidence from Treasure's declaration, he threw himself at Luit's feet.

'And the losses, sire. There are so many. Who will be next? Which one of us will be taken tomorrow?'

Another pushed him aside and took his place.

'Yes, sire, any of us that are sent run the risk of never

returning. How can we live with the fear? None of us can sleep anymore.'

And yet another barged his way forward and took his turn.

'They say you are afraid to go yourself, master. They say it! They say that you are afraid of what lies within the conduit and so send us instead. And many are being lost. Master, can this be so? Master?'

They all clamoured around him, their fears spilling out in a babbling flood of uncertainty and doubt.

Treasure broke the spell of his stare and dropped to her knees.

'See how the flock is filled with panic, sire. It is the curse! Your wife has brought it amongst us. She is the one to blame, sire. Rid us of her and the child and you will rid us of the curse.'

His eyes widened with anger.

'How dare you speak to me like this? How dare you?'

'Sire, this is a grim and loathsome place you have brought us to. We pay a heavy price to be wearied by endless time, to be soaked daily with the never-ceasing presence of eternity. That this overbearing evil will never be concluded is sometimes too much for us. But we are addicted to it, and your survival is essential for our addiction. Sire, you must not let the horror of our endlessness be stolen by change. We are both blessed and cursed by it all. You, sire, are our constancy, our guarantee.'

'Who are you to tell me this?'

'I am Treasure, sire, one of your most faithful. I have served you longer than any, given more than any—'

'Then you will lose more than any!'

Luit lunged at her in a fury. He grabbed one of her ears in one hand and her nose in the other. He twisted her head sideways. She choked and fought for breath.

The flock milled around them anxiously.

'Look! He is going to kill Treasure!'

'It is the curse!'

'What will we do if she no longer lives?'

'Help her! Help her! She speaks for us!'

'It is the curse!'

Luit held onto Treasure but the fearful words of the flock filled his head. He pinched her ear and nose hard as his anger mounted. She screeched. He saw the terrified faces of the flock. Even blinded by the redness of his fury, he could see that if his rage led to her death now, the flock would be in complete disarray.

Breathing deeply and fighting to control his wrath he managed to bring himself under control.

'I will not kill her! But my anger is too great to allow her to stay amongst us. The seeds of sedition she sets are a greater threat than the stories she tells. Listen to me! I am the one who brought you here. It is to me you owe your membership of my kingdom. I will send her out of your company. I will send her to Atho and there she can live out her years as an example of the rot of mortality. If any of you wish to join her say now! Speak now! Speak! And if in the future you are sent to bring your neighbour, or your son or daughter to join us, you will be able to see her and witness her slowly ageing, weakening with illness, and finally dying. On your return you will be able to report what you have seen to the others and you will all know that it is I alone who provide your safety from the destruction of time. Speak now, if you wish to renounce your claim on an endless future! Speak!'

They shied back, sniffing and coughing, shaking with horror at his proclamation, at the threat to their immortality, at the audacity of their outburst. The ones who had spoken wanted to withdraw their words but they were too afraid. They all backed off and tried to hide behind each other.

Slowly they dispersed as the rain became too heavy to bear. He watched some of them shuffling back to the fragile shelter of the dripping branches while others risked the downpour to get to the next beacon which struggled to keep alight. He felt the full weight of his responsibility for them and he bent under the strain of it. He looked down at Medean as she cradled the child. For a moment, he saw the child's hands and imagined them driving a dagger into his heart. He smiled at them both, turned and, still holding Treasure by the ear and nose, dragged her towards the conduit.

Luit found Lezma playing at the entrance.

'Look, master. I am on guard!'

She turned cartwheels around him.

'I say to anyone who approaches, "Who goes there?" and they must tell me their business. I would die before I allowed anyone to approach it, master. No, Lezma will never abandon her post. Look, master! See how I stand to attention! I am like a guard of honour awaiting your return!'

She poked out her small breasts—her nipples were hard and prominent. She grabbed his waist and kissed his chest.

'Lezma, dearest, faithful Lezma. I want you to take this woman to Atho. I want you to leave her at the entrance on that side and return alone. I have banished her from my company and from my kingdom.'

'It is done in a flash, lord. I am your speedy servant. Look! I have a rope ready to hold her by. Release her into my charge, master, and the job is as good as done. What next do you have planned for me? What is my next duty? Already I am anxious to undertake it. Lord! Lord! Tell me what you want me to do next. I am like a spring ready to jump to your service!'

'You are so eager, my little imp. Here, take her. I do not want to see her ever again.'

He released Treasure and she fell to the ground. Her nose was bleeding and her right ear hanging only by a thread of skin. Tears filled her eyes but did not flow.

Lezma wrapped the rope around Treasure's neck, pulled it tightly into a knot and yanked her towards the entrance.

'Time me, master. I will count the seconds myself. One, two, three...'

She ducked beneath the low entrance roof and yanked Treasure behind her. She was gone in an instant.

Luit walked slowly back to the beacon where he had left Medean and his child. The flock had never risen up like this before. He worried that his threatening outburst had been the right thing. He felt an unusual sense of isolation and disquiet. His body pained him and he made slow progress. Soon he realised that the flock were following him. They murmured and talked amongst themselves. One of them was pushed against him, but when he turned and hissed they fell back. Exhausted, he grabbed a woman, bit her hand and sucked her blood. It refreshed him enough to continue and the flock took some as well when he had finished.

Medean saw them approaching and was filled with fear. She jumped up, left the child and ran back into the trees. Luit shouted after her and, with difficulty, quickened his pace. The flock followed him, zigzagging in confusion, panic and disarray. Medean was terrorized, thinking that the flock had turned him against her and that they were seeking her life.

Blind with terror, she ran in circles—away from Luit's pleas to return, away from the flocks incoherent shouts and screams, and, in her frenzy filled mind, away from her own consuming fears. Finally, worn out and breathless, her arms and legs cut by sharp branches and thorns, she pushed her way into a tight entrance at the base of a small rocky cliff. She did not know it was the entrance to the conduit as she disappeared into the consuming darkness of its entombing labyrinth.

5. Treasure and Graf

Lezma dragged Treasure roughly by the neck as she ran through the passages of the conduit. Treasure cracked open her head as she was pulled headfirst into the sharp edge of a low roof. She choked as her lungs filled with water when Lezma dragged her through the long pond at the labyrinth's deepest part. Once Treasure became caught in a narrow fissure of rock and Lezma pulled so hard on the rope, and it tightened so much around Treasure's neck, that Treasure could not breathe at all and passed out. Lezma reluctantly loosened the noose at her neck but smacked Treasure in the face repeatedly to let her know how annoyed she was for being held back.

'Listen!' shouted Lezma as she stopped suddenly. 'Listen! I can hear someone calling. That cannot be so. No one enters the conduit without me! Listen!'

A faint cry echoed through the black passages—it was Medean, lost and hopelessly trying to call for help.

Lezma sniggered and grabbed Treasure by the throat.

'Now, I am going to leave you here. You can find the rest of the way yourself. I need to get back to my master to see what his next order is. See how I fly to him! I am a lightning imp!' She grabbed Treasure's head, held it firmly on the sides and twisted it to point towards only more blackness. 'Go in that direction and, if you are lucky, you will find the exit!'

She released her grip and, by the time Treasure held her arms out to try and locate her, Lezma had already gone.

Treasure crawled on, feeling her way in the darkness, falling into ponds of water, hitting her head and shoulders, clawing at the loose boulders as they fell from beneath her uncertainly placed feet. She could hardly breathe when, after several days, she finally collapsed on the inside of the entrance to Atho.

She stretched her hands forward and felt a softness— a cool pulpy surface against her fingertips. She drew back then pressed again—it was flesh, human flesh, cool and moistened with death.

She probed at it, locating limbs amongst it and prising them away one from another. She saw a chink of light and in its flickering and faint reflection she saw that a massive pile of bodies blocked her exit. Instinctively she turned back in revulsion towards the dark tunnel but realised straightaway that return to the labyrinth offered no way of escape; her only way was forward into the pile of flesh. She inhaled heavily, set her jaws tightly together and began. She struggled to move the limbs. Some were harder than others—cold and tightened by the solidifying blood inside their veins—some were more pliable, one or two were even still warm and seemed to tense against her efforts as she fought to free a way through them. The heads were heavy, lolling back on her straining hands as she battled to dislodge them from between the legs of others or from the contorted angles they had become fixed in. She used her own head as a ram and forced it between the tangled bodies until, bit by bit, she managed to squeeze herself between them. At last she stared up at the full light of Atho, but she did not have the strength to continue and she slept fitfully with the bodies pressing around her until the night passed and she found the vigour to carry on.

It was another full day and night before she could release herself completely and finally stand up. She held onto the side of the entrance and dropped her head back. The stench of death rose up around her. In one deep breath she inhaled the remembrance of her life on Atho and what had become the forgotten sharpness of mortality. In that single breath she realised that she would live only a normal span, that she would live it in the bright light of Atho, and that her mission in that life from now on would be to revenge herself on Luit and the evil he wrought in the shadow of his cause. She breathed in again. She wanted to inhale everything of Luit's other kingdom, his first home and now the breeding place for those he chose to bring to Athala. She loved the scent—not because of its sweetness, which was peculiar and heavy—but because of what it promised: freedom from the servitude of immortality, freedom from her slavery to Luit, freedom to act and revenge herself.

Unthinkingly, she stepped forward and stumbled on the contorted bodies of two naked women that still lay twisted around her feet. Their arms were intertwined, their fingers distorted, their heads crooked on broken necks. They had been dead some time—their skin was pallid and already tightening with bloating from infected growth within. The one's face was disfigured by a terrified anguish—sealed with the horror of her final moments. The other stared out wide-eyed, fixed with a vacuous innocence—as if she had passed beyond the terror of the other and simply could not believe what had overcome her.

Treasure struggled to push them aside but she was so exhausted she could not lift her legs high enough and so stepped on them, walking on the face of the disfigured one and the breasts of the other.

Another body was propped against the side of the entrance. It was another woman. Her legs were wide apart. Her succulent crack was soft and swollen, and blood seeped from its centre. Blood trickled from her mouth and ears. A bubble of frothing spit expanded between her lips. It blistered then burst. She twitched as the exploding globule splattered into a mist of red droplets over her chin.

Treasure pressed her ear against the woman's mouth and spoke.

'Tell me,' she whispered. 'Who did this to you?'

The woman's eyelids quivered. A glint of bloodshot yellowness flashed between them.

'Tell me who is responsible for this,' repeated Treasure. 'If anything can make your pathetic life worthwhile, it is telling me this one thing. Tell me and give yourself a place in the future.'

Another bubble appeared between her lips. It was streaked with red. It burst and splattered against Treasure's cheek. She rubbed it off and tasted it. It was sweet and enticing; her taste for blood was not diminished by her arrival in Atho.

Treasure grabbed the woman's throat and squeezed her thumb and fingers into its sides.

'Tell me! Speak! Speak, or I will throttle you and you will miss even your last breath of life!'

The woman choked. She gasped for breath. The beginning of a word came out with her painful, gurgling exhalation.

'Gr... '

Treasure pushed her ear hard against the woman's mouth. Another bubble of blood-streaked spit broke against it.

'Gra—'

'Speak!'

'Gra...Graf.'

Treasure tightened her grip in an involuntary reflex born of realisation. The woman's pale-skinned face reddened—a final surge of blood to her fading consciousness. Another bubble appeared on her lips. She sagged back. The bubble froze—it did not expand or burst. Treasure released her grip on the woman's throat.

Treasure looked behind her as if expecting to see something—an apparition, a message, a phantom leaping out from the distant past. She turned back and dropped her face between the woman's legs; it was as if she was seeking safety from a terrible threat. She pressed it against the soft flesh of the woman's wet warm cunt. Her lips opened against the fleshy softness. She reached her tongue out and licked it along the sweet crack. She lapped at it, probed it, sucked the fragrant moisture from it. She bit into it and sucked blood into her mouth. The woman's faint pulse was barely strong enough to pump her blood and drive it out of her sagging veins. Treasure drained the warm flow into her hungry mouth and gulped it down thirstily with greedy guzzling slurps. She let it smear over her face and dribble down her chin. After a while, when it became cool and thickened, she stopped. As she pulled away she gave a heavy long exhalation—satisfied with the taste and rewarded that she had not lost her desire to enjoy it.

With a great deal of effort, she pulled the woman free of the conduit and dropped her against the pile of bodies. Another groan was released from the woman's mouth as her chest smacked against the knotted limbs. Treasure sat on the ground panting. She pulled her knees up and leant back against the bodies—their closeness comforted her. She toyed with the limp fingers of one of them as she repeated the message from the still dying woman—'Graf'.

The conduit had been blocked by Graf, Luit's half-brother and sharer of Luit's own inherited evil. They had the same mother, and it was from her they had taken their power. Treasure had grown up with them both. Neither of their fathers was known. Their mother had said they were 'just men'. Graf was grotesquely deformed at birth. His arms were different lengths, his head oversized and his mouth surrounded by pulpy, blistered lips he could not close together. As he had aged, his hair dropped out in clumps and the teeth on either side of his lower jaw erupted and protruded through weeping holes in his cheeks. His mother hoped that death would save him from more suffering, but he did not die and his deformity increased. By the time he was a youth he could no longer stand straight and black matted hair grew in clumps from dark moles on his face and neck. His swollen knuckles touched the ground as he swayed forward with a heavy, uncomfortable animal-like gait. Although he could speak, his words were hard to understand. When he spoke he became frustrated with the isolation of not being easily comprehended and this caused him to slobber spit copiously down his chin and through the holes in his cheeks where his teeth protruded.

The two brothers had brawled over a girl when they were both young. Confronting each other on the south bank of Atho's central river and, with a crowd of others egging them on, it had turned into a vicious fight. Graf lost much of his sight that day when Luit had pushed his fingers into both Graf's eyes and punctured them. Graf had only escaped worse by throwing himself into the river and swimming to safety onto the other side. Luit could only watch—a fear of water having burdened him since his earliest childhood—as Graf scrambled up the opposite bank and crawled away to the derision and execration of all those that watched.

That day Graf left Atho and, driven only by resentment and jealousy, he roamed the surrounding wilderness far from the city. He was despised wherever he went for his ugliness and temper, found no fortune, and made only enemies. Forced out of every city and rejected by fear or disgust by every community he visited, he finally returned to Atho. His now uncontrollable and boiling bitterness was only made worse when he found that after his mother's death Atho had been transformed into a spectacular kingdom by the endeavours of his hated elder half-brother Luit. But he had nowhere to go and Graf—lonely, angry and disenchanted—chose the shame of remaining in Atho to the further indignity of leaving and facing more loathing from strangers in distant parts. At least, in remaining, his embittered purpose in life increased and so gave him a perverse sense of achievement. Luit, his own authority so much increased since Graf's departure, and with a certain degree of charity, tolerated Graf's remaining in the vicinity although not within the city walls.

Graf lived in a cave on an escarpment outside the city. He sat daily at its entrance in the hope of some good fortune or something that told of his half-brother's demise. But no luck came his way and he heard of nothing ill which befell Luit. Gradually, he lost any grip he may once have had on his sour reality. He killed rabbits and deer and because he did not know how to light a fire he ate them raw. In the winter he drank their blood for warmth. He became addicted to the taste of it and to the methods by which he could acquire it.

No one willingly visited his lair and his reclusiveness led to him becoming greatly feared. He took girls from the town, visiting it at night and stealing them from their beds or baths. No one was brave enough to attempt their rescue— even their own parents convinced themselves that their children had been lost or abducted by some unknown devil. Graf kept his captives in a cave deep in a forest. He fattened them on berries and fruit then, when his addiction allowed him no more restraint, he drained their blood into a bowl and drank it. Sometimes, if they had been starved long enough, he shared it with them. After a few weeks, if they did not die, he killed them because they were dried out and would yield no more blood. Sometimes, he hung their emaciated bodies like warning crows from the branches of trees. Sometimes he pinioned them to the trunks of heavy trees by driving a spike through the backs of their mouths. If they were still alive after he had done this he would sit at their feet singing to them in a cracked and tuneless voice. Some nights, when the air was still, his discordant crooning could be heard in Atho, even by people in their beds.

When Luit discovered Athala, and began to spend more time there, Graf became bolder. Every so often Graf walked in the streets of Atho. No one dared say or do anything to drive him out as half blind and ungainly he bumped into its walls and kicked out wildly at obstacles he tripped over.

Sometimes, when the cloudy wetness was too much for natural growth, and the flock in Athala were unable to sustain a harvest, Luit arranged for aid to be brought in from Atho. It was difficult to bring it through the conduit and sometimes, when there were arguments or disputes at its entrance on the Atho side, Graf took advantage, killed the carriers and stole the food. He would take it to the pink cliffs that stood facing east over the Atho sea and, with pictures of hatred for his half-brother in his mind, he would throw it

51

down onto the rocks below. As it was washed away with the receding tide, he imagined Luit desperately fighting his fears as he struggled helplessly in the waves.

Most of the time, Luit had come to ignore Graf's presence. But this ignorance only fed Graf's anger and resentment and, sometimes it boiled over. Graf seethed with hatred when visitors from Athala arrived in Atho. Some of them, when they returned with their brothers or sisters, carried cruel wounds that had been inflicted by Graf in outbursts of his jealousy and resentment. Unable to penetrate his half-brother's other world, Graf found satisfaction in trying to block the entrance to the conduit with the corpses of girls he had stolen from the town.

Treasure walked up the gravelled road to the city gates. She was seen at a distance and recognised straightaway as one of the first who had left many generations ago. A depiction of her was on a glass panel in the church and all who worshipped there were accustomed to seeing her image and associating it with their act of devotion. The gates were flung open to her as if to a visiting prince. People ran about the city streets, knocking on doors, rousing the sleeping, and excitedly announcing her arrival.

Treasure liked the air here—the smell of new mown hay, the fragrance of youthful girls, the freshness of spring. She stopped and inhaled it deeply. Naked young girls wearing only green garlands around their necks and crowns of white flowers on their heads lined the entrance between the open gates of the city. They pushed their hands between their thighs and bowed to her as she entered. She nodded to each of them individually and each was much excited by the attention. One ran forward and threw her arms around Treasure's neck. She pressed her naked crack against Treasure's leg. She moaned and squirmed in ecstasy. Several of the others ran forward. Treasure pushed the girl away and she fell to the ground. Treasure glared at the others. They backed off, looking down at their feet, shaking and barely able to hold back their exhilaration.

Treasure walked into the main square. Everyone bowed to her fearfully. She nodded to some, ignored others. Her instant celebrity surprised her but straightaway she adopted the air of authority that came with it.

The young girls pulled her by her hands into the church nave and pointed up to the meticulously worked image on the central stained glass window behind the gold encrusted altar.

'Treasure! Treasure!' they chanted. 'The pilgrim, Treasure has returned! The pilgrim is amongst us!'

They pulled her up the nave, past the altar and through a slit in the heavy ornate curtain that hung in front of the entrance to the vestry. They dragged her through a small door and back out into the streets where crowds surrounded her and applauded her return with unbridled joyousness.

Suddenly, everything went quiet—there were no clamorous voices, no clapping hands, no cheers, the birds went still and even the slight humming breeze went silent. The naked girls let go of Treasure's hands and ran and hid beside a nearby building. Others followed and with them the silence was broken, but this time the noise that returned was the sound of panic and fear as citizens grabbed each other and dashed from the open to find cover.

Treasure stood transfixed, alone in the middle of the street.

A shambling figure approached, his arms hanging unevenly, the backs of his hands glancing the ground. He fell sideways and stumbled, he felt his way along walls and hit the corner of buildings with his overlarge head as he made his way uncertainly towards the church. It was Graf!

He lifted his head and sniffed the air—he could sense her presence and her lack of fear. He opened his mouth as if to speak. A slobber of spit and mucous dribbled over his bottom lip and out of some of the holes in his cheeks through which his teeth protruded. A belching sound erupted from his mouth. He dropped his head and listened, as if his guttural utterance should have solicited a response. He edged forward hesitantly, holding his hands out to touch anything that was before him. Treasure stood her ground. Those that were hiding at the sides of the streets clutched each other tighter as Graf's hands got even closer to Treasure. Suddenly, he stopped. Her presence together with her lack of fear caused a wave of anxiety to spread through him. The very unusualness of the sensation caused it to happen again.

He swallowed hard and spit dribbled from the holes in his cheeks.

'We know each other,' she said. 'Do you recognise my voice?'

There was a pause. He cocked his head sideways and waved his arms from side to side as if worried that an attack could be mounted against him from any angle.

'No,' he spluttered.

'You should. Here, give me your hand. I will remind you.'

He offered his hand—it was dirty and his long fingernails were broken and yellow.

She pulled it towards herself, opened her legs and thrust its cracked palm between the tops of her thighs.

'Cunt,' he said in a quacking rasp.

She squirmed on his hand, opening herself and working two of his fingers between the fold of her crack.

Although it had been many years since Treasure's life in Atho, her youth had been preserved—her own moisture was still silky and its delectable scent still a fragrant delight.

She drew his hand away and offered it to his gaping nostrils. He sniffed roughly. He held it in his lungs, allowing her aroma to fill his body. As he breathed out, his red-rimmed eyes filled with welling tears.

'It is you!'

'Yes, and I have come back to you. After all these years, I have come back to be with you. Here, feel again, and you will know that I have kept my youth for you. My darling, I am still as young and fresh as when you drove your cock into me when we played together on the banks of the Atho River.

The tears streamed down from his barely seeing eyes.

'Treasure?'

'Yes. You gave up your sight for me and now I have come back to help you take your revenge. Graf, my dearest, earliest lover, we share a common purpose.'

'The world was younger then.'

'Even so, little changes.'

'But we are not the same.'

'In all ways that matter, we are the same.'

'But I am old.'

'It does not matter. You started from a disadvantage, Graf, and age has not marred you as much as those that had the benefit of natural looks and physique. Feel my cunt again, feel how it goes wet with your touch, feel how it yearns again for your misshapen cock. Feel how you still inflame me!'

He drove his fingers deeply into her flesh. She rose up on his hand, threw her arms around his crooked body and worked herself wildly up and down his thrusting fingers. She clawed her hands around his head, kissed him and ran her teeth along the raised veins that ran down his neck. His cock bulged out beneath his ragged smock and, when she reached down and grabbed it, it was so large she could not even encircle it with both her hands. She pulled herself from his fingers and tried to take it in her mouth put it was too huge. She lapped at it until his semen flowed in a massive downpour across her face. She scraped it up in her hands and drank it all.

In the end, panting and breathless, she spoke.

'Graf, you are an incomplete person—your disability makes you un-whole. But now you have found again your other self. I will complete you and you will be whole at last.

Go to your home. I will find you. Keep on with your work. I will formulate a plan and it will become our plan.'

He looked after her with longing as she turned away and walked back towards the church. As he left, falling sideways and stumbling down the street, those that had run for cover slowly emerged. They gathered around Treasure, licking at her face, covering her with flowers and kissing her body. She had faced Graf and he had left at her request. They led her to the church and sat her at the front of the altar—she had become their saviour.

6. The motherless child

Luit carried his child in his arms. He waited all night at the Athala entrance to the conduit for Lezma to return. He called a number of times but she did not appear. He felt angry at her slowness and troubled by the frustration of his wishes. He walked around in circles, his head bent, his limbs aching and tense. He looked up and saw a beautiful girl sitting alone on a moss covered tree trunk.

'Are you looking for your new wife, sire?' she said in a matter of fact way.

He approached her slowly.

'Who are you?'

'I am one of your flock, sire. Who else could I be? Aren't we all your faithful subjects?'

'What is your name?'

'I am called Cyrene, sire. Some say I am a fairy but I think I am not. Look! I have no wings! But the seed of eternity has set within me and my age is frozen. Would you like to see me dance?'

'What do you know of my wife?'

'I saw her running this way. She was running from you. Were you going to eat her, sire? Had you tired of her passion so quickly?'

'What do you mean she was running from me? How could she?'

'She *could* easily, sire—she was fleet footed. And the reason I say she was running away from you was that she *was*!'

He was angered by her facetiousness.

'Tell me why you think she was running away from me!'

'I do not *think*, sire, I *know*! She was afraid, sire, of being pursued by you and the flock. She ran up to me and told me so. "They are going to kill me!" she cried out. "They hate me because I am a foreigner, and he is going to kill me to please them!". She said you had a violent side, sire. She asked me if I knew of anywhere to hide.'

'What did you tell her? Where did she go?'

'I gave her the answer of course, sire.'

'And what was that?'

'That I did know somewhere to hide!'

'And where was that?'

'I showed her the entrance, sire, to the conduit. It was the obvious place, I thought. Do you agree? There, right there, that is where I sent her, into that entrance below the beacon you built when you first arrived. That is where she went, sire, into the conduit. She will not come out will she? She will be lost and die of starvation, or turn pallid and die of the darkness, or she will drown, or hit her head and bleed to death. Which one do you think, sire? What a waste, sire, all that blood dripping away in the darkness...'

Luit stood at the entrance and sniffed the air—he knew no other way of responding. It had not rained for a day. The air was heavy and expectant. Ragged figures toiled pointlessly in a barren field not far away; their efforts to till a small patch of sodden soil doomed to failure. He was overwhelmed with a deep sense of loss. Medean had gone. He felt empty.

'You could follow her, sire. You could bring her back. Nothing is beyond you, sire. Here, I will dance for you as you enter. Though there is a lot of water these days, sire. Look how stained the river is where it enters. It is so black! But that does not worry you does it, sire? You are not afraid to enter and find your loved one are you, sire? No, sire, *you* are not afraid of water are you? How could you be?'

He knew he could not follow her. His dread of the water, which he had conquered when he first explored the labyrinth, was now too great to fight; another penalty of endlessness—his growing fears. He shuddered at the thought of it. And anyway he knew that Medean was already lost—it was not possible that she could survive for this long alone without help. And he knew that it was not true that nothing was beyond him. This fairy girl was telling him what he knew but could not admit—he was afraid to enter; his fears were too great even to save the one he loved. He felt helpless and threatened as a new recognition came to him. Within the tone of this fairy girl's words he heard not the words of his adoring subjects but a half hidden criticism that reflected the deep anxiety of their world. Yes, he heard in her emphasis an echo of the anxious world of the flock and the usually unexpressed secret harbouring of a deep criticism of him, his weakness and his own lack of faith.

He placed the child carefully on the ground and grabbed Cyrene by the throat. She choked as he lifted her off the ground.

'Can you bring her back to me?'

She could not reply. She struggled for breath.

'Can your criticism make her return?' he shouted as he dropped her to the ground and kicked her in the hip.

'It...cannot...sire...cannot *make* her return...sire...'

He fell onto her, covering her body with his own as he bit deeply into her neck. Blood flowed from her veins as he bit chunks of flesh from wherever there was enough to grasp between his teeth. He tore at her, gnawing at her ill will and disaffection, snapping at her facetiousness and ready ability to expose his weakness. He felt as if he was punishing the whole flock for their faithlessness, their broken allegiance, for their lack of respect for his suffering on their behalf. She tried to speak but it was impossible. He ate through her neck until her spine was visible amongst the bloody mess of skin, tendon and muscle. In his feast, he was consuming all her words, the words of anyone who dared speak against him, who dared voice their criticism of his inadequacies. She was still gaping, blubbering, trying to speak, to cry out, to beg, but his own fears blocked out her appeals, and the taste of her flesh and the enjoyment that came with its flavour masked any response that might have ended her suffering.

He bit off pieces of her waist and hips but he did not consume them; he was ridding himself of anger, trying to wash away the idea that he had lost his lovely Medean through his own failings, trying to eradicate the idea that the flock secretly mistrusted him.

But even as he finished his torture of the girl he realised there was no peace to be found in retribution, there was no longer any comfort in the wet darkness beneath the heavy trees. His certainty had been shattered.

He went to the entrance beacon and found the child shrieking with hunger. He picked it up and could see only the image of Medean in its tiny face.

He called Lezma but still she did not come. For a moment, he thought she had abandoned him. Aimlessly, he walked a short distance to a collection of grey hovels the starving inhabitants of the flock called their village. Beyond was a broad mere formed where the sluggish river had broken its banks and flooded over the area enclosed by a wide loop. The heavy pressure of the hot, sticky air flattened its grey surface, like molten lead. Large barely submerged boulders of blue rock extended from the stark shore out into the water like the scaly back of a sleeping leviathan. Posts, fixed into the boulders, warned of unknown danger. Luit had once used them to impale dissenters who he had brought from Atho and who found they did not wish to stay. These days, taken over by the villagers, they were used to hang discarded rags as symbols of their fear and anxiety.

Naked children swam between the rising mounds of this rocky monster's back. They were its offspring, swimming between the outcrops it provided with its writhing body; it had adopted them as its heirs. Perhaps, in the distant future of endless time, when the behemoth gave way to others, these glittering water elves would inherit its empire. Or perhaps they would be destroyed and suffer writhing pain as flames consumed their heads long before they died in breathless agony—no one yet knew. For the moment, they pulled themselves up on the leviathan's shiny skin, stood ankle-deep in the warm water, and hung onto the banner topped crucifixes which stabbed its flesh. They held their hands above their eyes, waiting to ride the monster when it slithered away towards the horizon. They dived into the water and climbed out. When they emerged, tanned and dripping from their chins and elbows, they shone like stars. They pushed their hands back through their hair and opened their mouths wide. They pressed the palms of their hands together and skimmed the water away from their faces and mouths. It was as if their normal efforts to breathe again were not enough and they had to pray to be revived. They pushed each other, lifting their shoulders to counter each other's blows in a playful show of zestful and energized strength. But before any blow was seen through, and even if they fell and were off balance, they dived back into the water and swam to the next rising coil of the patient beast. One moment they were clustered in small groups on the boulders of its back, the next they were diving like arrows from its side. One moment they were ducking their heads beneath the foaming water, the next they were striking out for a fresh landfall beyond its next mounding horizon.

Amongst a group of four stood Lezma—older than the others but even more childish and playful. She rubbed water from her dark eyes. It ran in streams down her slender forearms and off the points of her elbows. She was the object of all the energy and excitement.

Luit cupped his hands around his blistered mouth and called out to her. His voice was low and hoarse. Persistent sores in his throat had changed his once clear timbre into a husky growl. Even so, it still carried in its broken tone the inflection of impatient anger that only accentuated his sense of loss, pain and anxiety.

'Lezma! Lezma!'

Lezma punched at one of the boys as his attention was momentarily distracted. She saw Luit and smiled broadly.

'Master! Master! I'm on my way to you!'

She dived from the boulder into the shimmering water. She pierced the water like a harpoon. It folded around her body with only the slightest ripple. She swam rapidly underwater and burst to the surface gasping for breath just before the shore. She sprang from the edge like a galloping seahorse and ran at full tilt to Luit. She stopped before him— panting, dripping wet, her dark eyes all the time flashing back to the boys who shouted and waved in eagerness for her return.

'Oh, master, I am a breathless imp. What is it, master? What must I do? Master? Master?' she nodded insistently, trying to prompt his quick response so that she could get on with her errand quickly and return to her play.

'Walk behind me, Lezma. Gambol for me. I need to feel your freshness. In a few short hours I have become more wearied than I can remember. I need your faith and your vitality. Let me see you cartwheel. The sight of your naked cunt may bring a thrill to me. I am so sorely in need of refreshment.'

'Will it take long, master?'

He turned and hissed.

'It will take as long as I say! Do not question me! I have heard enough of it today!'

She ran behind him, but her cartwheels were begrudged as she listened to the voices of the playing children fade into the distance.

They arrived again at the entrance to the conduit.

Cyrene lay on the ground, her naked body contorted in a mutilated tangle of fear and terror. Her blue lips were stretched tightly by a frozen scream. Her tongue hung limply to one side of her mouth. Her eyes had been gouged from their sockets and the two dark red hollows gaped unseeingly towards the heavy sky. The now drying drenching of blood—spilled as the flesh had been ripped without care so that Luit's tearing fingers could grasp the eyeballs and pluck them free—was cracking across her pale skin like the desiccated mud of an empty estuary. The youthful bloom that had once radiated from her smooth, fresh skin had ebbed, like a dried out riverbed, severed from its moistening

62

source and now doomed to parch in the withering heat of the sun. But there was no sun—only the leaden gloom of Athala. She had lost consciousness as Luit's fingers had reached into her skull, but it had not been her last pain. After he had dragged her by the hair across the forbidding entry to the conduit he had left her in peace. But it was not enough, he had returned. He had roused her and kept her alive as a pet, stroking her, pulling her behind him on a lead, rousing her and making her beg for more torment under the false promise of a rapid death.

'You must run another errand, little Lezma, it will not take long.'

Lezma looked down at the torn body of the naked girl and raised her eyebrows. She shuffled her feet and looked back in the direction they had come. Suddenly, the air carried the voice of one of the boys. It faded as she imagined him waving his arms frantically and calling her back to the water.

She pursed her lips impatiently and kicked at the bare ground with her toes.

'Will it take long master?' she asked absently as she looked up under her eyebrows and glanced back again in the direction of the sea. 'I have only just returned from my last task.'

Without warning Luit grabbed her by the neck and lifted her up onto her toes. Her small face reddened as she choked.

'My sweet little Lezma, you are so impatient. Perhaps I am endeared by it—perhaps not.' He held her there as he mused. 'Did you not hear me calling, my little imp? Oh, you must have done, I called so many times you could not have missed it.'

'Straight away, master. Like an arrow! I fly to you as soon as I hear the slightest sound. I listen out for you all the time, waiting like a runner, to begin the race back to you. Oh, master, I—'

'I know you take your own course. I have heard that

in Atho, it is not only my bidding you follow. I have heard that sometimes you fulfil your own desires. But my doubts are running riot. That cannot be true, can it my little darling? No, that cannot be true. You tell me otherwise, and you are my faithful imp, so it cannot be true. It is not possible that you would lie to me is it, my little Lezma?'

'Master, I—'

'Let us not waste time on this. This time, my little fawn, if you have any of your own needs you will not let them get the better of you. Yes, I am sure you will act only on my instructions. You are the only one I can depend on. And you will be with me again in an instant. Your little friends will still be waiting. Listen, there is the voice of one of them again. He is already greeting your return.'

He released his grasp and she fell to the floor coughing and holding her neck.

'Master! Have I displeased you? Should I not play with the boys? It is only a game. I do not mean anything by it. And I always follow your instructions. How could you think otherwise? I am your perfect little servant. I am Lezma, your faithful little imp. See how I tumble for you.'

She cartwheeled around him.

He laughed hoarsely. She was his only light.

He looked down at the body of Cyrene.

'I want to spend time with her as she finishes with life.'

Lezma stood at attention. She glanced at the twisted form of Cyrene at Luit's feet. She bent down and cocked her head to one side inquisitively. As she stared at the bloodstained face, the brow above the empty gouged out eyes furrowed in a slow gesture of hopeless pain.

Lezma jumped back.

'She is alive!'

'Of course,' said Luit, reaching down to the girl and stroking her tangled hair. 'I will rouse her completely when you have gone.' He laughed and blood-soaked spit dribbled from the edges of his blistered mouth. 'She may play with me a little more. Perhaps some of my joy will return with her companionship. I have sent for the flock. They can watch. She will be a lesson for them. Are you jealous of her, Lezma?'

'Your pleasure is mine, lord.'

'Lezma, without you my life would be worthless.'

'What must I do, master? What is my errand? Tell me and I will be at it as if I am a lightning flash.'

'Take that bundle of rags to Atho.'

'That is easy, master. I will be back before the boys can swim to shore.'

She ran to the rough bundle of rags apparently thrown aside. She picked it up and, surprised by the weight, she lost her grip and it fell from her grasp. A tiny arm emerged from the bundle. A weak cry accompanied it.

Lezma uncovered the small child. It was naked except for a silver trinket around its neck. Lezma smiled as the necklace sparkled in a momentary burst of sunlight.

'It is my own child; abandoned by her mother as she ran alone into the conduit. I cannot bear its presence now that my love has disappeared.'

Lezma reached for the necklace.

'I thought I was your love, master.'

Luit scowled at her.

'Think only of what I ask you, little Lezma. I will be rid of this child, but not here. I cannot risk unsettling the flock any more. Take it to Atho. These are your instructions—your precise instructions. Follow them exactly.'

'I will, lord. I will. I am your diligent servant. Always at attention!'

She stood before him, upright, her chin pressed down against her chest, her arms rigid, her fists clenched with her thumbs pointing downwards.

'Take it to a hillside away from the city. Nail it to the ground with this spike and watch it until it is dead. Ensure its necklace stays in place so that it is identified as mine.

Perhaps Graf will find it and feast on it. Or maybe wolves will eat it. I do not care. Its carcass will take its natural course once it has been exposed. I do not want to see or hear of it again. Do you understand what you must do, Lezma?'

'Yes, lord, exactly. It will be done exactly as you instruct. I will not even ask you why you want it done this way. I am simply your servant. And when I have done this can I return and play with the boys?'

'Make sure you are not wayward, my little imp. This mission is your most important ever.'

'It is as good as done, master!'

He had barely turned away and she had gone.

Luit grabbed Cyrene's red soaked hair in his hand and pulled her body behind him for a while. He dragged it back and forth across the entrance to the conduit as if trying to obliterate the loss of Medean and wipe out the insufficiency of his own abilities exposed by the flock's outburst of fear. But his keenness to give Cyrene more attention had sapped. He sat with her for an hour and simply watched her. Suddenly, all his interest gone, he pulled her vertebrae apart and cut through her spinal cord with his teeth and, as suddenly she dropped back limp and dead, she was at last relieved of the horror of living. Finally, he dragged her body up onto a rocky cliff and with a piercing shriek threw it down into the river. He watched it floating downstream in the black streaked water before turning and making his way again slowly into the dark wet forest.

7. Sharka

Lezma ran through the passageways of the conduit as fast as she could—she could not rid herself of the image of the boys waiting for her and her anxiety to return was irrepressible. She swung the ragged bundle loosely in her right hand and carried the hammer and spike Luit had given her in the other. She swam through the deep pond on her back and dragged the child, often its face beneath the water, at her side. When she emerged from her own exit into Atho she twirled the wet bundle around her head, held it high and ran across the grass as though she was bearing a banner into battle. She ran through the long grass of the meadows with the rags streaming from her hand, whooping and howling as if leading a victorious charge.

She stopped on a gentle hillside slope that rose above the city. After his mother's death, Luit had set about a reconstruction of the city to his own plans. He drew up a set of laws and all citizens had to swear their allegiance to the city, its rules and its leader. Those that could not accept these expectations were given no second chance and were straightaway exiled to the wilderness. He rooted out dissenters mercilessly, had them publicly flogged or humiliated, then driven naked through the streets and into the lands beyond the sphere of his protection. All that were banished were branded with a star on their forehead so that they could never enter the company of his chosen citizens without notice. Many tortured souls, bearing his newly burned brand, turned their heads back to the city as they left uttering oaths of vengeance, cursing every second of Luit's existence and wishing on him the horror of continuous pain.

The city stood on an easy rise amongst fertile undulating hills and was encircled by a heavy stonewall. Lookout points were built into the wall at regular intervals and manned at all hours so that those exiled could not regain entry and outsiders could only come in by invitation. Towers of some of the taller buildings were visible from a great distance. Immigrants were drawn from the surrounding area by the sight of these tall edifices, believing that in their shadow lay wealth and fortune. They gathered at the base of the walls and each year Luit held a court in which they could present themselves for admission. Those that were not chosen were branded and banished. Looking out from the city walls of Atho, its inhabitants seemed like insects as they toiled with their daily chores in the fields before returning again to the safety of the city before nightfall.

Lezma unwrapped her package. The naked child spilled out onto the dew-wet grass—it was sodden, dirty and sleepy from exposure and lack of food. Lezma poked it in the side with a pointed finger and rolled it over a few times like a cat would with a captured mouse. It made no sound. Lezma knelt and drew its heels together. She held the iron spike above them. She pushed the point against the child's pale skin—it gave easily. She held the spike firmly in place and lightly tapped its end with the hammer. The sharp point first indented then just punctured the child's skin. Blood trickled from the wound—light red, a tiny flow. Lezma smiled broadly—pleased with her achievement, and her obedience to the task set her so precisely by Luit. She held the head of the hammer squarely against the top of the spike, drew it back again then, without any further thought or consideration, brought it down heavily with a hard and determined smack.

The first blow drove the sharp spike straight through the child's lower legs, splitting the tender pale skin and shattering the soft new bones. The second sent it further, driving it deep into the hard ground and pinioning the injured helpless child. The tiny victim did not squirm or twist—it did not know the root of its pain only that its body was filled with it. Its mouth opened wide. At first there was no sound—it was too shocked. Its eyes filled with tears and transparent mucous ran from its mouth, then, as the silent pause crossed the threshold of unbearable suffering, it cried out.

Lezma hit the spike once more, threw the hammer

down and jumped to her feet. She danced around her prey, running in wide circles, whooping and howling, then running back and skipping over the suffering child. She cartwheeled and turned a springing somersault. She rolled in the grass. Dew glistened on her back. Her act had enervated her, and her extra eagerness and vitality elevated her into a world of pure joy. She fell to her knees, bent over and lapped at the blood that now ran freely from the injury she had so keenly inflicted. She rubbed her face in it then quickly jumped up and sat at a distance on a raised clump of moss. She breathed heavily, unable and unwilling to release the waves of pleasure that her cruel act had spread unreleased throughout her trembling body.

Lezma looked down on the city. She licked blood from her lips and wiped her blood-smeared face with the backs of her hands. Its scent filled her nostrils—she could not resist its thrilling tang. She ran back to the child and buried her teeth into its hip. She sucked at it eagerly—drinking from the crying baby, supping the crimson liquid from its rapidly exhausting form. As she drank, her own saliva ran into the child's wounds. Drawn in by its weakly beating heart, it mixed with its blood and infected it with what its attacker was—an acolyte of her prince, a carrier of his germ, a living form with a singular lust for blood.

The child screeched as its blood felt the shock of Lezma's infection. It tightened itself in a hopeless throe of resistance then, as the germ flowed more freely in its system, it breathed deeply between its cries and provided oxygen for the foreign cells which now flowed freely through its veins.

Suddenly, as the grip of ecstasy slowly released her, Lezma caught in the corner of her eye the glint of the trinket at the child's neck. She made a grab for it but, as she touched it, she snatched her hand back, shocked by the fiery pain that contact with it transmitted. She edged her hand forward again but left it shaking on the brink—unable to get closer, unable to stand the stabbing pain that touching the jewel had given her. It was as though contact with it would burn her skin away—as though it would split her skin and expose the white of her bone as she held it. She pursed her lips and scowled. She was not sure who was the enemy—the child for having possession of the trinket, or the trinket itself for threatening her harm. She curled up her index finger and forefinger of her right hand and pinched the child's nose tightly between their knuckles.

She jumped to her feet and ran in bounding circles around the child. She howled and smacked the palm of her hand against her mouth to break the sound off and force it into a rhythmic syncopated dirge. She threw herself down and rolled on the grass again. Her pink nipples hardened as her breasts were covered with sparkling drops of morning dew that glittered on the grass. She spread her legs wide and pounded the palms of her hands on the ground. A glistening line of the faintest moisture glowed in the delicate crack of her cunt—she ran her fingers along it and rose up against the joy released by the contact they made.

She jumped at the sudden sound of a voice.

'You want it don't you?'

Unsure of where the voice came from, Lezma reached out and again felt the sting from the trinket. She pulled her hand back and nursed it in the other.

'Yes. Yes.'

She looked up and saw Treasure standing above her. She jumped to her feet, whooped for joy and ran in a circle around her.

'I can get it for you. It is within my power,' said Treasure.

'Yes! Yes! I must have it! What do you want? A favour from my master? Anything! I can get you anything!'

Treasure stared at the child.

'I will take the child.'

Lezma stopped suddenly. She heard Luit's words in her head, his expectations and her own promise to him that she would fulfil them.

'For the trinket? And I will be able to hold it?'

70

'Yes, I will take the child and you can have the trinket.'

'Take it then. It means nothing to me. It is as good as dead anyway.'

Lezma held her hand out and squinted up her eyes as Treasure dropped the necklace into it. It did not burn her! Treasure smiled as Lezma ran in wild circles swinging the trinket about her head and howling excitedly at the top of her voice.

'It is mine! It is mine!'

Treasure pulled the stake from the ground and the child with it. She carried the barely breathing baby, its fractured legs still pinioned by the stake, and walked down the hillside towards the town. She did not even glance back at Lezma who ran frantically around the fragrant green meadow swirling the trinket around her head in boundless joy before disappearing like a phantom into the darkness of the conduit.

Only the barest trickle of blood dripped from the baby's wounds as Treasure took her back to what had become her new home in the church. She placed it beneath an icon of Luit—a resemblance of him as a young man— filled with vigour, energy and pride at the achievement of building the golden city of Atho which was portrayed at his feet, dwarfed by his titanic stature.

'Let this image burn into your mind,' she chanted over the child. 'I have saved you for one purpose only, to be my agent of destruction and bring to an end the reign of evil which stalks the rotting horror of Athala. You, my little one, will achieve what no other can. Look up at the image above you. You will be the bearer of his death. You will be the bringer of mortality. Your tiny hands will drive death into the evil heart of the one that now looks down on you. You, small as you are, will be the living vehicle for Luit's fate and the embodiment of my own revenge.'

Treasure squatted beneath the looming image. It caught Luit at his most proud—at the handsome zenith of his

71

good looks and charisma. It was an image filled with confidence, with zeal and intention—it portrayed the greatest energy and the highest level of commitment to a convincing good that can be found in a man. It was a portrayal of pride based upon the belief that pride was a quality of reality.

Treasure pulled up her skirt and opened her knees. She showed him her cunt, widening her thighs as she felt the certainty of his gaze fixed on the moist crack at its centre. His confident stare inflamed her, drew her in, and increased her need to show her contempt for him. She pushed her fingers along the crack, opening it, releasing more of its moisture. She slipped them along its silky furrow and each movement back and forth released a fresh wave of urgency and desire.

She concentrated on his eyes—it was them that fixed her interest, that probed her flesh, that made her want to open her whole self up to him, to release everything that was pent up inside her away from his presence. Each slow movement bred more fixations—she felt bonded with him, caught in his gaze and locked into it like a prisoner, captive to his will and held there until only the final rush of her joy would set her free.

She increased the pressure of her fingers against the slit of her cunt. The silkiness of its soft edges thrilled her whole body. She pressed against her clitoris and shuddered as the intense throb that arose in it filled her body. She muttered in time with her efforts, at first challenging him, telling him of her hatred, then espousing her love, her unquenchable desire, her need and her yearning. She called out to the icon, demanding it reach out to her and drive its fingers into her cunt. She shouted for them inside her cunt, her anus, her mouth—she wanted him as part of her, she wanted to feel the confusion of intimacy, the loss of one to another that derives from abandoned sexual complicity. She dribbled and shouted, she racked her body with punishing thrusts of her fingers and responded with harsher movements in response. She dropped her buttocks to the ground and felt the cold marble of its surface against her skin as she raged at him to fulfil her needs; each booming cry reinforced her pleasure and built the anticipation of fulfilment that blended perversely with images of her own revenge and Luit's eventual suffering.

Eventually, already exhausted by effort and anticipation, she fell back overtaken by her own ecstasy. She lifted her hips high and kept plying the furrow of her flesh, but there was no longer any need—she had drawn out the depths of her need and it was overflowing without any aid or support. She dropped back—a used up victim of her own pent up expectations. But she still shouted out and writhed and it was an hour before it finally let her go. When in the end it freed her she fell on her side, gasping for breath, her heart pounding. Her body still jerked as the shocks of what she had brought out still fought against dying down and resisted earthing themselves into the world around her.

Slowly, as her body began to relax, the young girls who attended her gathered around and started pawing at the child. Its blood now barely ran; its breath was so slight its skin had become blue. The girls were too young to know how to attend to its needs but they saw that the stake needed removing from its legs, that it needed nourishment, and that its cold body needed warmth. One of them pulled at the stake—the wretched child was too weak to even whimper at the rough treatment. Another held the baby by the head so that there was enough purchase to slowly drag the stake out of the fractured legs. The girl who removed it sniffed at it as if that would somehow tell her something of its origin or original purpose. One of them held her nipple to the child's mouth and as it tried to suck from it the others giggled. They all took turns until one of them brought a cup of milk and drained it over her fingers into the child's hungry mouth. They covered it with a blanket and when they returned to it the next day it was still alive.

Treasure chose one of her subjects, Dagan, to look after the child. He had brought up three younger siblings as a

73

child when his parents had been banished by Luit and had learned how to feed and care for them; indeed, he still tended to them and they depended entirely on his efforts. Treasure told him it was a great honour to care for her charge and that in return, as well as the benefits of extra food and clothing for his family, sometime in the future, she would expect something special from him. She made him swear with his hand against the icon of Luit that he would not betray his promise to her. Treasure told him that the child would stay in the church beneath the icon of Luit every night but that he had complete control over how it was fed and cared for, and over where it went in the day. She would tutor it, she said, when it was old enough to learn from her. She told him it did not have a name and that if it made his task more amenable then he could name it.

Dagan worked in the fields. For some time he had fought in a small band on behalf of Luit when some of the banished had tried to return and take control. He was both tender and strong and the best times of his life had been in the service of a strong lord who demanded physical strength and mental fortitude of which Dagan could supply both in abundance.

He made some tiny splints and bound the child's legs against them. Each day he checked them and adjusted them if necessary in the hope that when the child grew it would not be handicapped in any way by this early assault on its fragile body.

Weeks after he took charge of the child he had still not given it a name. He asked some of the women in the city but they came up with nothing that either pleased him or he felt suited his charge. One night he dreamt of a female warrior called Sharka. He loved the image that appeared in his mind, an unconscious reverie where he worshipped his elegant mistress and followed her faithfully as she travelled across hostile lands without fear. When he awoke he went straight to the child and named it after the heroine who had appeared to him in the night.

The child soon grew strong. Its early setbacks were not even memories to those who knew her as she formed into a beautiful sinewy youth with bright blue eyes and a mass of tangled straw-coloured hair. Dagan tended to her always, protected her in the early years and was always available to come to her aid as she matured and forged her own way in the world; he was her servant and protector, and was completely devoted to both these tasks as he was to her.

She always slept beneath the image of Luit. When she was three, Treasure began her education and each day Dagan escorted her to the small room behind the altar curtain of the church for her daily lessons. It was indoctrination. Sharka was shown the image of Luit and programmed in hatred of it. Treasure thought of little else, her only aim in life to breed Sharka into a tool for her own ever-increasing loathing and bitterness.

Sharka took on much of what she was taught, but she always retained something of her own personality, her own need, her own sense of freedom. As Treasure's instruction intensified Sharka never lost track of the existence of something beyond that which she was taught—she knew little of what it might be, but she knew it was there and she knew it was a counterpoint to the single view of existence which Treasure was daily feeding her. In the evening Dagan sat with her and told her of the wilderness his parents had been banished to and of the dream in which he had seen her image and learnt her name. Subject to these two influences, Sharka became a polarised personality: she had a dark and deeply set compelling purpose which she did not understand, and she had an inspiration of a world beyond the confines of her daily routine in which she believed she could express what little she knew of herself. She was naive and delicate yet single minded and filled with blackness. If she saw a spider creeping across the floor she would poke at it, as would a cat. When she felt the tickling sensation it caused on her skin she giggled, then she would smack her hand down with a sudden and frightening need to finish its life. Dagan saw the danger within her and knew it was uncontrollable.

During Sharka's childhood years Graf deepened his compact with Treasure. She went to visit him regularly outside the city and told him tales of his half-brother, his success, his authority over the flock, his unbreakable control and power, and his immortality. She told Graf that it was at his expense that Luit had prospered and that as long as Luit remained successful Graf would never achieve any happiness or satisfaction. She taught him that Luit was the sole obstacle to him finding a life that could be anything like satisfactory. He crouched before her, spit dribbling from his mouth and running from the raw edged openings in his cheeks, rocking from side to side, seeing in his bleak mind the images she conjured up of Luit's death and destruction. Everything in his world hinged upon his half-brother's downfall, upon rising out of the morass into which he considered Luit had banished him.

Treasure watched him as she poured her own hatred into him. She watched him dribble and moan in an ecstasy of expectation as she made up pictures of Luit falling before Graf's feet, begging for mercy and forgiveness, praying for a compassionate death at his hands. If she saw his damaged eyes wandering to the side, perhaps for a moment his attention being taken by something else, she grabbed his hand and thrust it between her thighs. She pressed her cunt down on it and covered it with her free running moisture. He would always respond, lifting himself clumsily towards her, feeling her flesh roughly, lifting his ragged smock and exposing his throbbing erection. She would lap at its tip and make his semen flow and, when he fell back breathing heavily and jerking with pleasure, she would resume her commentary and her convincing images would fix themselves even deeper in his mind.

As the sun went down she would leave him and return to the church in Atho where she would continue with her propagandising of Sharka, holding her in her arms, crooning to her and repeating her hatred of Luit before the icon that Sharka was made to sleep beneath.

Graf would wander around the countryside, sometimes finding a girl to enslave, sometimes returning to places where he had girls strung up in trees, or sometimes simply going to the dead pile at the entrance to the conduit and repositioning the bodies he placed there. Treasure's indoctrination bred a new sense of purpose in his life. He keenly searched for bodies just to build up the pile at the entrance, knowing that the denser and more prohibiting his blockage, the more problems the dammed water would be in Athala. He did not know that his edifice of corpses, which held back the waters, was for the moment saving Atho from the germ that now flowed in the contaminated river of Athala. He did not know that for a while he was saving Atho from the corruption of the blood and saliva of the flock as, starved of a good supply of blood, they fought each other to drink from the ever blackening waters of the river.

Sometimes Graf visited the cemetery in Atho and dug up bodies. He carried them or dragged them to the entrance of the conduit and wedged them into the pile of corpses. He took great pride in placing them carefully, wedging their limbs between any gaps in the bodies already there, or lacing them together in ways that strengthened and bonded the fleshy edifice. Often he worked all through the night, slipping between the bodies, inhaling their staleness, sometimes chewing on their flesh to replenish energy lost by effort. Sometimes he fell clumsily from within the pile and dropped into the conduit. A large pool was backed up behind the dam he had constructed and he fell into it with a massive splash. His poor sight meant that being in the darkness hardly affected his abilities, and he swam to the opposite shore with ease. He climbed out of the rancid water and stumbled around feeling his way along the walls. He cocked his head from side to side, marvelling at the quietness and the icy chill that hung around his wet feet. Even when he was parched and thirsty he found it impossible to drink any of the foul water.

One day, he slipped down the inside surface of bodies and slid into the water. He choked as its acrid aroma filled his gaping nostrils. On the other side of the pool he laid on his back, imagining his victory over Luit, the expression on his half-brother's face as he met his defeat, and the way he would desecrate Luit's body when finally he had stopped gloating over its end. Suddenly, he heard something—a plaintive howl, the weak call of a desperate woman. He called back and immediately the howl grew in strength—the caller making an extra effort in response to the recognition that her voice had been heard. He called again and again she responded. Her voice got closer and suddenly he felt Medean's hands on his half blind eyes!

She could not see him and so ran her hands across his face to gets an idea of whom and what he was. She felt his disfigured eyes, his loose-lipped mouth, the horrifying holes in his cheeks where his teeth protruded. She did not wince or pull back. When he grunted she was not repulsed and when he put his clammy hand between her legs and pushed his finger into her cunt she did not resist.

He found a rope and tethered her to an anchor of bodies on the inside of the conduit. He brought her food each day and sometimes fed her himself by hand. All the time she remained in the dark. She could no longer face the light. Her skin was pale and papery. She had been three years trapped in the conduit. She had fed on scraps of food dropped into the stinking water in Athala by disgruntled members of the flock, and had chewed on the remains of rotting bodies tossed aside by the disdainful Luit. She had lost touch with the light, with the taste of food, with an awareness of her own body. All she knew was the nauseous stink of the water and the forbidding darkness. All the time she tried to speak to him, but his replies were difficult to understand and in the end she made do with silence. Most days she felt his face and sometimes she allowed him to penetrate her cunt with his massive penis.

When it became obvious to her that she was pregnant she tried to tell him by rubbing his hands across her swollen belly, but he seemed unable to understand and, after the due course of time, she delivered the child herself in the water that reached out in a blackened pond from the edge of the dead pile that its father had constructed from the bodies of those he had killed or salvaged.

8. Lezma's exile

After leaving Luit's child with Treasure, Lezma ran through the conduit quicker than ever before. Unable to see in the inky darkness, she ducked and dived in accordance with her memory of the geology or the number of paces or skips between certain memorised points. Counting out loud, she swam the required number of strokes and jumped out on the shores of ponds and meres before she even knew her feet were on the ground. In no time at all, she burst like a shooting star from the entrance to the conduit on the Athala side. It was raining hard but there were blue patches in the sky and through them shone piercing shafts of light. It penetrated the falling droplets and cast several patchy rainbows one of which reached down to the edge of the mere where the behemoth lay. Without pause, Lezma ran down to the broad mere and where the rainbow fell she threw herself into the water with an arm spread explosive splash. The boys clambered around her noisily and she swam from them and led a wild chase between the curving backs of the leviathan that still rested lazily near the shore. She stood up on one of the twisting mounds and like a banshee howled at the top of her voice. The boys joined in and when their voices built to a deafening crescendo, they all jumped into the water clutching each other in an entangled joyous bundle of limbs.

She played all day—harder than ever before. The rainbows came and went, slowly changing their angle, their length and their intensity. Lezma and the boys were dappled in the multicoloured light that reflected from each of them as if every one of them was a living prism. As the day began to lose its light, and whimpering with exhausted bliss, she stumbled up along the shore, crawled beneath the protecting arms of a massive oak and, still glistening with water, fell asleep.

She slept deeply, dreaming of the boys and of running through the sandy shallows with them. She pictured having a lasso cast over her head and being dragged through the deeper parts in a splashing, arm swirling turmoil. She thought of it tightening around her neck and she wondered how long she could hold out without taking a breath. She listened to herself counting—'One, two, three, four...' Suddenly, she awoke. She reached to her neck, expecting to find the tight pulled noose and discovered the locket gone. She must have lost it in the water! Her stomach filled with anxiety. She sat bolt upright and looked around.

'Lezma! Lezma!'

It was Luit calling her. He sounded angry.

She jumped to her feet and ran towards his voice. As she came closer and saw his face she realised her error—she had not reported to him straightaway. He would not greet her with joy this time. He would not stretch out his hands, lift her high and draw her close to his chest. She knew she had done wrong; she had strayed and been too wayward. She stopped short and dropped her head, biting her lips and kicking at the ground. She did not know what to say or do— she felt caught out and unable to defend herself. She looked up nervously.

Luit pondered the small silver locket in his hand. He dangled it from his fingers as though he did not want it too close to him. He swung it slowly on its fragile chain. The smooth surface glinted as an unexpected shaft of light touched it. It was impossible to tell where it came from: perhaps the glitter from a spluttering beacon placed high above the trees; perhaps the glint of a distant star beckoning this shabby sodden world to join it in its glowing death; perhaps the yellow beam of light cast by the flickering torch of a wanderer, hopelessly searching amongst the snarled roots of trees for a natural flower and driven deeper into the night by the chants and execrations of those of his flock that would expose him for his folly; or perhaps, even a glint from a momentary shaft of sallow light that dribbled from the transitory dying sun as it curved laboriously and mostly unseen above the leaden skies of Athala.

Luit's eyes remained fixed on the dangling locket as

he cocked his head slightly to one side and curled up the edge of his mouth in an uncomfortable smile. It was as if he was listening to it entertaining him with a joke, favouring him with a secret about another, whispering an intimacy which only they could share because they were confidants or because they were the only two alive who shared a common language. His broken lips tightened, his smile changed and his face became troubled and quizzical. The entertainment had passed; it had not fascinated him for long. Now, it was as though he wanted to hear something serious: some news, something that would signal the start of a new life, some clue that would provide him with enough hope and novelty to make the passing years of eternity less tiresome, less dark. This creature, this man, this time-worn fallen god, condemned to witness all eternity, was hungry for something fresh, something new that would make at least the moment worthwhile.

Lezma dropped to her knees before her master.

'I have come as quickly as I could, master. I ran like the wind. See how breathless I am. I huff and puff like a dragon! Look! I could scorch the ground.'

She dropped forward onto her hands and breathed hard across the wet grass.

'Master! I could set the whole land on fire!'

He tossed the locket upward on its chain, holding it tightly between his fingers as he spread his upturned palm beneath it. It fell back to the centre of his crinkled hand. He curled his fingers round it, slowly closing them on it then squeezing it rhythmically as if wondering whether or not it would squeal under the increasing pressure.

'Look, my little fawn,' he growled, releasing his grip on the locket and holding it up on its chain. 'Look what I have found. A trinket!'

Still on all fours, she looked up under her eyebrows and bit her lips. She had not lost it in the mere. Luit must have found her asleep and removed it from her neck.

'Oh, sire, you have saved me. I thought I had lost it.

82

You see everything. You always make everything alright for your little imp.'

'Lost it? You said you had lost it?'

She suddenly realised what she had said. It had not been hers to lose!

He opened the clasp of the chain and held it open, making it ready to fall like a noose about the neck of his impatient elf as she jumped to her feet.

'Please,' she said as she stretched her neck out eagerly, unable to hold back from trying to regain the possession. 'Please, master, thrill me as you adorn me with your gift.'

He snatched the chain up and a dark petulance of disappointment spread across her face.

'So you recognise *my* locket, little Lezma?'

She bowed her head seriously, but smiled capriciously as soon as he could not see her face.

'Of course,' she giggled, expecting him to forgive her, lower the chain and make it his gift.

'Good,' he said lazily.

Lezma's expectant face lit up with relief. He had forgiven her! Again, she reached towards the chain to welcome it about her narrow, straining neck.

'Of course, master, of course,' she said excitedly. 'I am ready for your gift.'

But as she stretched forward he snatched it away a second time and held it behind his back. She thought it was a game and she ducked to find it, lifting her shoulders and moving her head from side to side, beaming broadly and laughing with joy when he confused her by dangling it in front of her then snatching it away a third time.

He lowered his gaze and she stopped as her nostrils filled with a sudden thickening of his scent. He inhaled deeply, unable to suppress his anger any longer. She realised it was not a game. A rain soaked bird, startled by something unknown, flew in terror from somewhere amongst the tops of the dripping trees. Lezma's face lost its smile. She shrank back and began to tremble with a deep and unstoppable sense of foreboding.

'Your task was simple my glittering child, and yet you failed me. Not because you were unable—perhaps I could have forgiven that—but because you were unwilling. That is so much worse. That is unforgivable. Your own desires overcame you. Is that not so, little Lezma? Your own will was more important than my wishes.'

'I *meant* to do what you said master. I really did. There was something in me, something fighting me. It was a demon of some sort. Yes, master, I was possessed by a demon, but I have fought him and beaten him. I will never fail you again, master. See how I have vanquished the evil spirit that took control of me.'

'Little Lezma, you thought you could deceive me. Did you really think that was possible? Have you not felt my presence always? Surely you did not think there was a time when I was not with you?'

Lezma felt the enveloping darkness of his anger. She felt trapped and cornered.

'Master, please, another chance. Give me another order. I will not fail you again. Please master. I will spear that demon through the heart if he ever shows his face again. See, master, my hand is ready—'

He was overshadowed with a heavy cloud of blackness. He could not bear her faithlessness—he relied on her so much.

'There are no more chances, my little elf. Poor Lezma, you have failed me. You should not have let my trinket stray into your hands. I told you it was important, and now the moment is lost. Now, there is nothing more for you, no more smiles, no more deceit, and no more blood. For you, my sweet imp, there is only suffering. Your faith to me, like your promise, was just a shadow, and now you will spend eternity in its shade. Dearest Lezma, you know I cannot forgive you this time. You know I cannot bear to have you close to me knowing that you have broken your faith.'

She looked down at her hands—they were shaking; she could not stop them. The greasy light reflected something from her skin she had never seen before—the pale translucence of death. Suddenly, she realised that death would be her end—her endless future had been taken from her. She saw how easily innocence could be corrupted. She hung her head in shame. She knew that no repentance could win her pardon, that there was no clemency for her deceit—eternity had withheld forgiveness, she was damned to annihilation. Her hands shook more. She was terrified by what she must now face—non-existence, an end to it all.

He took her trembling hand and walked her to the entrance of the conduit. She did not look back as the boys ran up from the lakeside and called over to her, asking her when she would return.

'Goodbye,' Luit said curtly; he did not even use her name.

She felt damned, un-absolved and forsaken. She stood at the entrance shivering—her gleam had gone, her shimmering light dulled by his rejection, her glitter clouded by her knowledge of a lost eternity at his side. For a brief moment she saw her life, a flash of something intangible, a fleeting image that would not stay still, but as quickly as it appeared it was overtaken by a growing black horizon—the endless reaches of darkness that heralded the coming of never-ending nothingness. For a moment, she wondered what death was like, but she realized it was not like anything. How could nothing be like anything? How could nothing be experienced? Death was an experience of the living not part of the existence of the dead—the only knowledge of death was in the thought of it. Death was only in life; it only existed in the living world, in the realisation in life of her own permanent absence. She could not fear that which she could not yet know, but the rationale did not prevent the abyss of dread that opened up beneath her. She felt as if she had stepped over the brink of a fathomless black pit.

85

'Go,' he said. 'Never return. I can stand no more deceit. Wrap this around you, it will be colder for you now.'

He passed her his black cloak. It was almost too heavy for her to hold and she struggled to pull it around her shoulders.

He knew he did not want to exile her from his company—it was a terrible thing to separate himself from her. But what could he do? He was being compelled by an imperative that was not of his making. He was responding to some absolute value that he knew did not exist but which had to be obeyed. In truth, he wanted to bring her close to him, to feel her liveliness and vitality against his suffering body. He wanted to chide her and see her laugh. He wanted to see her frolic for him and fill him with delight. But he knew he was compelled by this powerful and suspicious force to remove her from his presence. It was like punishing himself for something he held to be of little consequence; he was compelled to act virtuously by a power he had to obey.

Lezma knew her life was now forever changed. Of all her desires this change was the least wanted. More than anything she wanted to stay with him, to serve him, to bring him pleasure and amusement. But, as Luit was driven by an absolute idea, so she knew her transgression meant the penalty had to be obeyed. Something universal had proclaimed her deceit as out-of-keeping with faith—it was unforgivable and the sentence must be accepted.

She faced the entrance to the conduit, opened her arms and spread them into a sudden gust of heavy damp wind. The weighty cloak was caught in the gust and billowed out like a black sail. The wind pushed her forward and her form, shallow and un-shadowed, faded quickly as she walked slowly into the darkness of the labyrinth.

'Lezma!' he called.

She turned, thinking he was calling her back, thinking that he had forgiven her. Of course, he had forgiven her! Her heart was pounding with excitement.

'Master?'

'The child is dead, is it not?'

This was just a final test, she thought.

'Oh yes, master, the child is dead. You know I do everything I am told, master. I staked it to the ground as you commanded me. Whack! Whack! Whack! I am your loyal and obedient servant, master.'

'Then go.'

Her heart sank. The idea of a reprieve was stolen in an instant.

He watched after her, filled with emptiness and despair. He knew he was rejecting the only one who loved him, but he could not stop himself—the feeling of faithlessness and treachery had overcome him and he had acted as a victim of a quality that was formulated beyond and out of his reach.

As she stepped heavy hearted into the darkness she seemed to become transparent. He knew her immortality was leaving her, that in a few more steps the weight of the heavy cloak would be too much for her to bear. He wanted so much to bring her back, he wanted to see her eyes brighten as she ran to him, but he could not find any forgiveness in himself—it had been stolen from him by the same thief that had taken his darling Lezma.

He sniffed the air and inhaled her sweet aroma. She did not look back as the heavy forbidding rock of the conduit entombed her. Her form was enveloped by the blackness; it became amorphous and dissipated as Luit inhaled one last regretful waft of her lemony scent until only the scent remained.

He dropped down at the entrance to the conduit and wept for several days. Many of the flock gathered around him and murmured and whined as their fears grew commensurate with his loss and lack of confidence. He had realised immediately that Lezma was the only one except him who knew the route through the conduit, and that his fears barred him from even entering it. He felt suddenly trapped and cut off. It was as though he had sliced his body in half.

He sent two of the flock to follow her, to call out to her and let her know that he had forgiven her, but they did not return and after a week were presumed lost. Their loss increased the flock's insecurity and their feeling that Luit's action in exiling Lezma had brought them more harm, bred a grumbling resentment that undermined the shreds of weakening confidence that were left. He gathered them all together and spoke to them. They stared at him silently with empty eyes and his hopelessness was only increased. He did not know how to fetch fresh blood from Atho and the flock was on the edge of collapse. One day he thought he heard Lezma calling from the labyrinth and he told them that they were to expect her return. But after a week she still had not returned and his failed prediction and obvious inability to summon her caused even greater fears to spread. Eventually he wandered out of sight of the beacons and if he saw any groups of the flock he went back into the forest to avoid contact with them.

Lezma cast off the black cloak at the first opportunity. She trampled on it in the darkness of the conduit, shouting at Luit, condemning him, vouching her hatred of him, and repeating oaths of revenge and loathing. She ran first to her own exit on the Atho side. She looked down from beneath a tussock of moss on the hillside above the main entrance and watched Graf slaving at repairing the pile of bodies. She threw some clods of moss down on him and giggled when he looked up hopelessly to see the cause. She ran down to him and pranced around him, skipping and hopping as he struggled to make out her darting form.

'I am Lezma! An elf!'

He reached out to her clumsily and tripped on his own feet as she spun around him.

'My! You have a big project here! I could help you if you wish? Perhaps my old master would come and assess your work?'

'Old master?'

'Yes, Luit.'

Graf stared hard at her.

'Where is Luit?'

'In Athala. And I have left him.'

'When will he visit again?'

'Never. He is too afraid. Perhaps you will be the new king in his place?'

9. Sharka leaves Atho

Sharka developed into a beautiful woman—tall and graceful, blue eyed, and focused. Her lithe limbs were well formed with clearly defined muscles and she walked with only the slightest limp from her childhood injury at the hands of the covetous Lezma. Because of her relentless conditioning by Treasure, she held an intuitive hatred of Luit and the flock, and from the stories that Dagan told her, she nurtured a sense of adventure and wonderment at what lay beyond the city walls. Treasure was her oracle and her proclamations were like the blood that flowed in Sharka's veins. For Treasure, Sharka was a vehicle for her own vengeance. Sharka held Dagan in the highest regard—as if he was her father, or knowledgeable elder brother. Dagan worshipped her as if she was the embodiment of all that could be wished for, all that was beautiful and to be admired. Sharka shared her time between both her mentors but if both called at the same time then it was to Treasure that she ran. Faithfulness, naivety and dogmatised teaching meant she believed everything Treasure told her. Sharka's personality had thus become polarised. She had a temper and a temperament that tolerated no middle ground; to her some things were right and others wrong: the right she accepted, the wrong she rejected—the right she upheld, the wrong she smashed. If Treasure told her that something was abhorrent and should be destroyed then she would destroy it without question or regret. Sharka's view of what was right or wrong had neither absolute value nor rationale upon which it rested but had either been taught her by Treasure or picked up piecemeal from her own restricted experiences.

Treasure taught her of the flock, their shambling hopeless ways, their need for leadership from Luit, their anxiety, and their hunger. She told her how they lusted for blood and resented their master for not supplying enough. She told her how they drank the water of the river and infected it with the saliva they dribbled back into it as they slobbered at its edge to quench their thirst. She told Sharka that it was her mission to eradicate Athala of them so that its waters could flow pure again and once more nourish the meadows of Atho. She told her that the only way to kill them was to decapitate them, stake their severed heads on pikes, set them on fire and mutilate their bodies. Only while this was happening and their leader was sufficiently distracted would he fall victim to the knife. When all was done, they must be buried together in a pit, covered in lime and left to rot. Another must never touch Luit's body again, and no part of anything he had formed in the world must ever contact his rancid flesh.

Sharka sat cross-legged at Treasure's feet as she repeated the instructions. Even before her early childhood began to pass, Sharka knew them exactly and carried a precise picture in her mind of their completion.

When she was strong enough Dagan introduced her to the sword. She used a wooden one for a year, mastering the techniques of distance, timing, cutting and thrusting. When she was strong enough he had a fine two-handed sword made especially for her by Atho's best blacksmith. It was heavy and she had to train hard in order to wield it. With determined perseverance and extra training to build up her muscles, she was soon able to handle it. She learned how not to hold the grip too tight and how to use her leading arm for strength. She learned a reliance on footwork and how to combine any defensive movement with an equal movement of offence. Dagan drilled into her the belief that she should only use her skills fully if the odds against her were at least three to one. She built strong muscles but it never altered her litheness and slim elegance. She became fleet and quick and never looked more comfortable than when she was prepared to take on adversaries. He took her to kill deer and taught her how to be unfeeling as she drove the blade into another living thing. For Sharka the lesson was easy—she had no sympathy for any creature and did not hesitate to bring life to an end.

'Does it feel anything?' she asked as she pushed the blade of her sword slowly into a fawn's throat.

'As we do, I suppose, mistress.'

'So this young fawn feels the same pain as I would?'

'I think so.'

'But I have trained myself not to feel pain. Can this creature do the same?'

'No, mistress, it is only an animal.'

'It looks at me as if it is trying to tell me something.'

'It is because you are its killer, mistress. It wants to share its last moments with you. They are its most valuable.'

'But I do not understand it. Teach me, Dagan.'

'The language of the dying is one language. Everything that dies speaks in the same tongue.'

'Tell me.'

'This fawn says it is sorry to die, and sorry to die at the hand of another. It would have preferred to grow into a buck and spring around the forest looking for a mate. But it has resigned itself to death already. It looks at you knowing that you have also saved it from any further suffering.'

'What suffering?'

'Any hardships, but especially living and knowing that it would die at a future time. You have saved it from living with the knowledge of its own death.'

'Why is that such a good thing? Surely we all know we will die.'

'We do, yes, but there is a difference in knowing it and knowing it for yourself.'

'And does this fawn not now know this for itself?'

'No. Mistress, it only knows that it is dying now. It has not prepared for it in any way. And to be unprepared for death is a good thing.'

'Then it will thank me for its death?'

'Yes, mistress, it will.'

'And do I know for myself that I will die?'

'I do not know, mistress, only you can tell that.'

'I do not think I will, Dagan.'

'Then maybe you will not, mistress!'

When they returned from the forest, Dagan made Sharka a leather scabbard to hang from her belt. She carried the sword in it during the day and, even though she propped her sword nearby where she slept at night, she kept the leather scabbard secured to her belt and the belt firmly around her waist at all times.

One day Treasure took her to the shore of the sea to the east of the city. It was the first time Sharka had seen the sea and, although Dagan had told her stories about adventuring sailors and islands that lay beyond its horizon, she had no idea what it was truly like. When she saw it she was terrified—the expanse of it, the heavy rushing noise it made, its surging ebb and flow, the infinity that it expressed. Above all it was exposure to the sheer mass of it and the fear that it would consume her, drag her down breathless into its depths and subjugate her with its overwhelming power, that made her pull back in panic. Others from Atho were there, all young people taking a break from labour in the fields, swimming and enjoying the warm summer's day. Dagan was amongst them, taking pleasure in their youthful company and the vigorous play that came with it.

Sharka sat high up on the shore on the edge of the dunes, as far away from the water as possible. Treasure sat with her, chiding her about her fear.

'Look, my sweet, look at your servant, Dagan. He swims like a merman! Why do you not join him? He would raise you up on his shoulders and you would feel the back of his neck against your flesh. Think of that, my darling Sharka—the feeling of your slit open and bare against his skin. What would that make you want to do, my sweet?'

'I would squeeze my legs around him until he was throttled!'

Treasure rocked back laughing.

'Is that all you can think of doing, my sweet?'

'Is that not the right thing? Is that not the right way to use my body—to dominate the bodies of others, to withstand

and be victorious, to bring death? That is what I have learned with the sword and in the way I kill things. That is what you have taught me.'

'Yes, but a body has many other uses, my sweet. Your legs can entwine a man in many different ways?'

'Tell me how.'

'Have you not seen the wenches in the fields? Have you not watched them writhing with their skirts up and with men between their legs? Have you not heard their screams of delight? Have you not seen their gaping wild abandon?'

'Yes, I have, but I have thought nothing much of it. I assume it to be a game. I think perhaps they are wrestling!'

Treasure fell back again clapping her hands in amusement.

'Yes, they are wrestling!'

'Then I am right. The game is that one is the beast, the other the hunter, and only one can be the victor. I am right am I not?'

'No, my sweet, it is victory over a different beast than you imagine.'

'Tell me of this new beast. I must know how to slay it.'

'I have left this part of your education aside for long enough. It is time for you to learn a little more about this wrestling! Look! What do you think of that fine young man who has a young woman standing on his shoulders? Look how he balances her! Look how he grips her ankles! Look at her delight! Listen to her screeches!'

'She would lose her delight if she fell and he kept hold of her ankles. She would drown! She is entirely at his mercy and should be fearful.'

'Not so, the power is with her, my child. Watch and you will see how she exerts it. This young man may look stronger and appear to have control, but let us watch and see if that is actually the case. There is something to discover here about where power actually resides. It is a lesson which you must now learn.'

'There, she has fallen. I was right! Now, if he chooses to hold her ankles she will surely drown. Yes, she is splashing in panic. I am right! Treasure, I am right! Look, she is fighting for her breath!'

'Watch, my child, sometimes outcomes are not so instant.'

'She will drown! I know she will! Look! She is upside down and clawing at his body with her hands! She is trying to climb back up him but her head is still under the water. She will soon feel the bite of water in her lungs! He has her! Yes, she will surely drown!'

'You are not attending. Look, my child. See how her rump is exposed. See how she bends her legs and offers what is between her thighs to his mouth. She climbs up him with purpose. She is not trying to escape the breathlessness of being beneath the water; her intention is to defeat him by offering him something he cannot refuse.'

'What cannot be refused? Surely there is no such thing!'

'There are many things we cannot refuse, my child, and one especially which a woman possesses and a man cannot do without,'

'What is that?'

'See how this woman offers her rump closer to his mouth. See the delectable folds of skin; the parted flesh at its centre that is her cunt. Can you imagine its scent? Even in the thrashing salt water of the sea its fragrance is a delight, it attracts the man like no other scent. Look, he is already seized by it! He has been distracted by it. See how he loosens his grip on her ankles. See how his mind mislays any other sense of purpose. See how the sight and scent of that beguiling flesh draws him closer to defeat.'

'But he has her! I can see it. Her thrashing is lessening. She does not have enough breath to continue. If he can just hold on a little longer he will have beaten her.'

'But he cannot, my sweet. See, his tongue is already lapping at her flesh. He is a bee licking up her pollen. It is a sweet flower impossible to resist. He has already lost. See, she has pressed herself closer. His tongue is inside. He has let go his grip completely. She is rolling him on his side and coming up for air. She is gasping fresh breath, replenishing herself, tasting her triumph. She is rolling him over now and he is delving her flesh deeply with his tongue. He cannot stop himself. She is wrapping her thighs around his head. Now he is hers to control, she has won, she is the victor and everything that has been done has been on his part. Look, his face has disappeared beneath the water as his tongue chases her flesh. He will not be parted from her fleshy cunt, he cannot bear to take his tongue from it—it is his entire world, his obsession, his mania. She needs only to keep her flesh beneath the water and he will drown because he can think only of keeping his tongue inside her. His own life has become irrelevant.'

'Treasure, I don't understand. She has done nothing.'

'But she has everything that he wants, my child. Imagine the taste of her sweet moisture, the silkiness of her open flesh, the tugging of her passion at its entrance. His world needs nothing else.'

'It is mysterious.'

'Think of your own crack, my child. Think of how it opens at the slightest touch, think of the glistening of fragrant moisture along its edges. Think, my sweet. Inhale its scent.'

'I do not understand.'

'Think of the scent, my sweetness. Think of the moisture that runs on your fingers when you prise your own beautiful slit apart.'

'It is a heady aroma indeed. I feel my own desires increase when I breathe it in.'

'It is that desire which is at the root of this man's downfall. She has used his desire to defeat him, my child. I will show you. It is an easy skill to acquire because it needs no training; it is simply a matter of realisation. And it is a realisation you will use to great effect because you are naturally beautiful and desirable. With this *and* the sword there is no enemy who can stand against you. I will give you a lesson. Dagan! Dagan! Bring that young man to me. Drag him from the cunt of that young girl and bring him here. Dagan! Prise him away from her flesh and bring him to me!'

Dagan broke away from his play and grabbed the young man by the ear. He hauled him out of the water and dragged him up the shore to Treasure.

He held him there, the young man's head at an uncomfortable angle as he tried to wriggle out of Dagan's grip.

Treasure got up and started poking at him with her long fingers.

'See, my child. Look at what protrudes between his legs. See his cock. See how it is hard, see how it throbs and stiffens.'

The young man tried to squirm free as Treasure cupped her hand beneath his penis.

'Do you know why it does that, my sweet? Why it lifts and throbs against my hand.'

'No, I do not.'

'Because of hope, my child, because of hope. That is what drives a man, hope. And I will show you how to use this hope as surely as if it was a sword in your hand.'

'Madam, should I force him to his knees?' asked Dagan breathlessly.

'No, Dagan. Let him stand for the moment. He may choose differently in a while. Clasp your hands over his ears. I do not want him to hear what I say to the lady Sharka.'

Dagan clamped his hands over the young man's ears. Blood flowed from the gaping hole in the one where it had been pinched through. His eyes were wide with uncertainty. His muscular naked body dripped with water and shone with the crystals of drying salt as he stood in the warm sunshine. His erection was still burgeoning and solid, the shaft of his penis long and straight. His testicles hung heavily at its base, and the glans at its tip was swollen, dark pink and beating

97

with irrepressible expectation.

Treasure pulled the back of her hand across her mouth and spoke to Sharka.

'Undo your waistcoat, my child. Yes, take the buttons apart. Do not rush! Take your time. See how the young man's eyes follow your every move. He is wounded, captured and held deaf by your servant, and still he is entranced by the simple act of you undoing your buttons. How can this be? Do you wonder that? Look at his cock! See how it throbs even more in response to the work of your fingers. Now, open your waistcoat and let it fall to the floor. Yes, like that. Press out your breasts, let your beautiful hard nipples strain against the material of your blouse.'

'Is this right? Am I doing it right?'

'Yes, my sweet, it is perfect. Stand a while. Do nothing. Breed hope. Even my cunt goes wet at the sight of you. Now slip your blouse over your head. Lift it up, stretch your arms, let him see your ribs, the definition of your muscles, show him how your breasts are tautened by the way you reach up. Yes, lift it over your head. Let him look while your face is covered, let him see you as if he is observing you secretly, as if he is peering through a half open door or an uncovered window. Now throw it down, let it fall to the ground easily. Expose your breasts fully to this hopeful young man. See how he licks his lips in anticipation. That is the hope I told you about. It is overcoming him. It is pent up inside him like a bubble waiting to burst. It has expanded to its limit. Dagan! Release him!'

Dagan pulled his hands away from the young man's ears. The young man did not take his eyes off Sharka's breasts.

'Now, my sweet, tell him to kneel before you.'

'But I have not beaten him, and he does not know me as his mistress. Why should he do that?'

'Tell him, my sweet. Tell him to fall to his knees before his mistress. Have faith.'

'Young man, kneel before me. Kneel before your

mistress.'

Without hesitation the young man dropped to his knees, clasped his hands together and looked up at Sharka.

Sharka giggled at his obedience.

'See, my sweet, he is like a dog. Now undo your belt. Slip it from the buckle and pull it from your waist. See how his eyes hunger for you. See the glisten of saliva on his lips. Look at his throbbing cock! Look at its size! Wouldn't you just love to feel it in your mouth? My sweet, ask him how faithful he is to you.'

Sharka giggled again.

'Speak, young man. Are you my faithful servant?'

'I am, mistress. I will serve you until I die.'

Sharka's eyes widened with excited joy.

'Now, my sweet, pull down your hose. Show him the crack of your flesh. Rub your fingers along it. Show him how it glitters with your moisture. Show him the glistening wetness on your fingers. Yes, like that. Show him the sweet scented and sparkling film that covers your fingertips, let him sniff it, let him think of tasting it. Now, widen your legs a little, not too much, just enough for him to see. Yes, yes. Now ask him how much he will serve you.'

Sharka looked down at the man.

'How much will you serve me, young man?'

'Completely, mistress. I would give my life for you.'

'See, my sweet, he is yours, you have defeated him and he is your slave. His desires have made him your victim. Now tell him you want him to fulfil his promise.'

'Will you do that, young man? Will you give your life for me?'

'I will, mistress, without hesitation.'

'Here, my sweet, hold your sword at his throat and ask him again.'

Sharka gripped the massive handle of her sword in both hands. She pressed the tempered point against the young man's throat. She looked down at his throbbing penis.

'Now, as I hold this against your throat, tell me

again.'

'I would give my life for you, mistress, without hesitation.'

'Now, my sweet, take him at his word. Act now!'

In one heavy thrust, Sharka drove the sword into the young man's throat, out from the back of his neck and into the ground behind him. He did not move and was in an instant pinioned by it. His eyes still looked at her glistening crack as, in his last few bubbling breaths, he repeated his devotion to her. His prayer of loyalty complete, he died and his lifeless body hung on the sword which Sharka continued to grip tightly in her hands.

'See, my sweet, how he submitted to you. He was yours completely, and he died happily at your hands. His desire was more important to him than life itself. Remember this lesson. It will be the way you will defeat our greatest enemy. Kill through combat if you must sharpen your taste for death, but if you are faced with a stronger opponent breed hope on your victim's lips before you slay him. Now, let us dispose of this handsome young man's body. Dagan! Dig a grave in the dunes and we will be rid of him and then you can return to your entertainment!'

Slowly, Sharka drew her sword from the man's neck. He rested on his knees for a few moments then slumped sideways to the ground. She bent to his body and cupped her hands beneath the still bleeding wound at his throat. She let it run into her hands and when it was full she brought it to her lips and slowly drank it all.

'A victor's right,' said Treasure with obvious pleasure.

Sometimes, when Treasure was visiting Graf, or Dagan was called away because of sickness amongst members of his family, Sharka was left by herself. Lacking purpose, she would walk down to the seashore, sit high up on the grass-covered dunes and look out over the restless waves. The world that she had been educated in meant that all things had a place—there was no alternative to this; her created personality did not allow for correction. She was not immune from fear and her polarised world meant that all the potential she had for fear was distilled into one place. This distilled fear was of water; it was as though the horror of its nature was innate—a part of her very self. It rained rarely in Atho—its main source of water for drinking and irrigation was its river—but when it did she took shelter and, even protected from it behind the thick walls of the church, she found herself ill at ease, shivering and gasping in short panicky breaths until it stopped. Sharka often challenged her fear—such a challenge was combative and had a purpose—but she never vanquished it.

As she sat in the dunes she imagined walking down to the water's edge, feeling it around her feet, her knees, her breasts, her neck. But the more real the pictures became, and the closer she saw herself to it, the more her panic set in. She felt her pulse throbbing in her neck, and her lips drying with her quickening breaths until, in the end, she succumbed to its victory over her and turned her mind to something else.

One stormy day she sat high in the dunes looking out to the east. She watched a heavily sailed trading yacht approaching the headland ahead of a dry stormy onshore wind. Cresting waves built on the surface churning it up into a great white mass. She had heard of the vessel's mission from some of Treasure's servant girls. It was bringing a platinum bell to Atho from a distant land keen to offer its most prized possession in the hope of forming an alliance with the more powerful Atho. They said it had been cast by a master craftsman but had never been sounded. They did not know the reason why its tone had remained untested and there were rumours that evil itself had been thrown into the furnace that had fired its ingredients.

As Sharka watched, the wind picked up. The captain bellowed orders but the wind bore away his words and the crew were left in leaderless confusion and fear. Drawing on their experience, sailors fought to reduce the canvas that pulled the vessel heavily on its side in the crashing waves. But their uncoordinated efforts were unsuccessful; one was tangled in a tightening sheet as it was whipped taut by the thrashing canvas, and two others who tried to release him were tossed overboard. Some of the sailors on deck hung onto the gunwales and shouted more unheard commands, but their cries were meaningless. The wind exploded into an overpowering tempest and the boat foundered on the gnarled black rocks and broke in two.

The crew were thrown into the water and caught in a swirling vortex caused by the fierce tides and the curved nature of the rocks. Some of them saw Sharka sitting on the crest of the shoreline and cried out to her for help. Their plight caused her own fears to overspill and she could only stare at them, as if they were images reflected on a wall, players that were not part of the real world, as though they were marionettes or merely the dramatic puppets' jerky shadows.

As she gazed at the drowning men an ungainly figure hurled himself into the water from the rocks and swam out strongly to them. He ignored their grasping hands and shrugged off their desperate pleas for help as he fought his way through the maelstrom to the wreckage of the boat. She watched him crawling up the wretched bodies of those that still clung to the fractured wooden hull as if they were a ladder, and she watched him wrench the large bell from the sinking boat's central wheelhouse. He attached one end of a long length of rope to the ring at its top, and the other he wound around his waist. He threw himself back into the boiling water and struck out for the shore. He snatched at the rope and the bell rolled from the swamped and broken deck of the boat. As soon as it touched the water, its weight dragged it straightaway to the bottom of the churning sea. When he reached the shore he laced the rope around a prominent rock and, bearing strenuously against his feet that he pressed flat on the rock's base, bit by bit he managed to haul the bell clear of the water and onto the rocks.

Sharka watched him rubbing its glittering surface with his forearm, murmuring to it and caressing it. He rested for a while, then tied the rope around his body again and laboriously dragged his prize away across the rocks and into the stormy darkness.

Sharka stayed where she was watching the men drown one by one. Each one faced his death differently: some with silent resignation, some with terror, some fighting against it as though even with their last desperate gasps they believed they had a chance of survival. She watched their bodies swirling around in the maelstrom and forming into a raft as if, even in death, they were bonded as comrades in need of each other's company and companionship. She stood as if to go to them, to swim out to them and bring their bodies to land so that they could be buried, but instead she turned and walked through the dunes back to the church in Atho and her sleeping place beneath the icon of Luit.

10. Jewel

One day Treasure woke Sharka and commanded her to leave Atho.

'Go into the wilderness with your servant, Dagan, and gather together a band of followers. The flock are many and much effort will be needed if they have to be searched out, and much appetite for killing will be necessary when they are dispatched. You will need to teach your chosen band precisely how to do this, for to be certain of destroying them it must be done in a special way. But remember, my sweet, the leader of the flock is yours alone to dispatch.'

Sharka replied as if she was reciting a poem from memory.

'And my victory over him will be a product of his desire. When I drive my sword into him he will be longing for my body and will have abandoned all thoughts of his own safety.' She stood before Treasure like a soldier before his commander. 'Have I remembered well?'

'Yes, my sweet, that is exactly it. Now go.'

Sharka nodded obediently, strode out of the church and walked into the main square. Dagan was already waiting. Treasure had roused him earlier, told him of the plan, promised that she would not only provide food and shelter for his family in his absence, but that some of her young girls would attend to them as servants.

Sharka climbed up onto her horse and, with Dagan riding beside her, left the safety of the city walls.

They rode for several days from sunrise to sunset. She never looked back; her mind was focused only on her mission.

As they got deeper into the countryside they were surrounded by increasing signs of decay: streams and sluices were silted up and choked with weeds, vineyards were overgrown, and fields were either barren dust-bowls or soppy quagmires. The contaminated excrement of Athala, seeping through the pile of bodies at the conduit's entrance had begun to infect the very soil of even the kingdom's most distant parts.

'The land is not so good here, Dagan.'

'No, mistress, it is lower here and easily swamped.'

'Find me somewhere where the banished live.'

'It is here before us, mistress, Oskia, it is their stronghold.'

Sharka and Dagan rode up to the shambling assortment of buildings housing small disparate groups of dissenters and their descendants banished by Luit from his city years before. It was surrounded by a moat along the inner edge of which was a roughly built and poorly maintained high wall.

Frantic servants pulled at the chains that held the heavy drawbridge. It clanked loudly as the iron banded wooden structure creaked and strained on its massive rusting hinges. Dagan dismounted and held the reins of Sharka's horse as she waited impassively for the bridge to be fully raised. She stared up at the high walls, fixing the men who patrolled them with her hard stare as Dagan pulled her horse forward and over the still dropping bridge.

It was dark behind the drawbridge, as though it had been built to keep out the light. Sharka stood in the centre of the broad litter-strewn square. She looked around assessing the natural features, calculating the numbers of inhabitants, their qualities and any likely threat they may present. Most had run into the shadows of buildings or hidden behind walls or carts.

Sharka pulled at the reins in her hands. Her horse spun, champed its hooves noisily on the ground, snorted loudly and came to an uneasy rest.

'Listen, inhabitants of Oskia, I bring you the news you have been waiting for. I bring you news of your own salvation. I bring you news of your own chance at revenge. How many years has it been since the tyrant Luit threw your ancestors out of Atho? I see some of your older ones still bear the terrible brand he inflicted on them, and that the rest

105

of you carry a copy of it to show your allegiance to their suffering. What a terrible mark it is for you, and a dreadful remembrance. But at last it is the time for action. I am here, your new mistress, Sharka, to bring you the news of Luit's destruction. Follow me and I will lead you to his lair. Follow me and you will be able to revenge yourself on his flock. Follow me and you will be present when I alone will take his evil life. Everything we find you can have. All booty is yours, nothing will be held back. I want none of it. All I ask is your faithfulness and your commitment until the act is complete. If you can give me those two things then I will ask no more. Are there any here who wish to follow?'

They came out from their hiding places, trying to make sense of what she had said, or already making agreements with each other if they thought they had understood her right.

'Yes, I will,' shouted one raising his hand high.

'And I.'

'And I.'

A group formed around her, thrusting their hands into the air, all keen to take part in her venture, seized by its prospect and with at last a chance for revenge against the one who had cast them out into the wilderness.

'Do you accept my terms? Faithfulness to me, and commitment to my cause?

'Yes, yes,' they chimed.

'I repeat, that is all I ask. If any one of you breaks that oath I will kill him. Be clear, I have no mercy. Take me at my word in everything. Now, we will stay here for a month and Dagan will train you in how you will dispatch our enemy; the flock may be weakened but they can only be killed in a certain way. Go with Dagan. I need to sleep.'

The month passed quickly. They were eager to learn from Dagan and keen to submit to Sharka's authority. Two of them decided against continuing and Sharka had their legs broken with a heavy hammer so that they would not be able to follow them or go to anyone else with news of their expedition.

Dagan reported that their training was complete and they were ready to leave and, on her instruction, he would assemble them in the square.

An hour later she sat on her horse before them. She nodded slowly as if in prayer.

'Do you affirm your faithfulness to me and your commitment to the cause which I have laid out before you?'

'Yes,' they said in unison. 'We do.'

'Then we leave!'

As Sharka pulled at the reins of her horse and turned its head to face the open drawbridge, an old woman moved out of the shadows and stood before her, blocking her way.

The old woman's grey hair fell in sticky tangles around her heavily lined face. Her mouth drooped sideways pulling the edge of her fleshy lips at an angle and puckering up the loose skin that hung in pleats on her brittle bony jaw. Her companion crouched by her side. He was old and wizened, and still clearly bore her great affection. He held onto her arm, comforting himself with her closeness and her with his warmth. He had adopted the role of wizard and constructed himself in its image with his inky black hands, his long fingernails, shaggy hair and rough unkempt beard. Both of them bore the original brand of those banished from Luit's empire in Atho, and both carried the resentful look that had been burned into them the day the red hot irons had been held against the sizzling, pain racked skin of their foreheads.

Sharka stared at the old woman and ignored her fawning curtsey.

'If you do not know, I am the Lady Sharka. Why do you block my way? What is your name? And the name of your feeble companion?'

'My name is Jewel, lady, and this is Julian—he is my servant and my wizard. How powerful I am to have such a potent servant. Can you see how strong he once was, how fleet of foot, how able, how potent?'

'I see only a frail old man who can barely walk and clutches onto you to prevent himself from falling down.'

'You should look beyond what you see, lady. That is where the truth is.'

'I have been here a month and have not seen you. What do you do in this forsaken place?'

'I plan our revenge, lady. That is the sole purpose of our lives.'

'Who is it that you bear such a deep grudge against?'

Jewel opened her mouth to speak and spit dribbled out of the corner of her downturned lip. Julian bent his head and licked it away.

'Surely, you don't need to ask, mistress? The lord of Atho, of course, the one who scorched these marks into our flesh—the evil Luit.'

'Then what lies in your future also lies in mine, for I am committed to follow the same path.'

'I know nothing of the future, lady. I see only the past. It is sufficient to tell us what will happen in the moments ahead.'

'Ah, that is just your age. You have seen too many seasons. I can see it etched in your wrinkled face. The old always look back. It is their only world.'

'No, I see what you call present as only in the past, and I see the future being consumed incessantly by the darkness that it brings.'

Sharka jumped from her horse, squatted down in front of Jewel and looked hard into her eyes.

'Then what do you see in this shadowy world, hag?'

'I see only repetition, only decline and the spiralling of future into the dark history of the past. It is so dark there—unremitting, incessant, as though light has been obliterated. But there is a trail of brightness. That is what you must follow—the trail of light that is smudged in the darkness. It will be the path to your destiny.'

Sharka looked dismissive. She pursed her lips.

'You tell me nothing I do not know. What you

108

describe is the fate of all mortal things. And what trail of light is this?'

Julian leant across to Sharka.

'Let her spread the runes, lady Sharka. What she says may be clearer.'

Sharka pulled the black fur of her cape around her neck and sighed.

'Very well, spread your runes, woman. But I warn you, I am keen to leave and am impatient of seers and oracles!'

In one slow move Jewel cast her runes upon the floor.

Julian put his face close to Sharka's ear and whispered a commentary to her in a slow singing melody.

'See how they spill from her fingers, lady, like tokens from her old heart. Watch them tumble, like jesters in the court of sadness. See the madness settle on their numbers, flickering scales of blue and green. Listen to them gossip in the misty shadows, murmuring low their troubled meanings. Now see how, slowly, from the light around them, mingling with the magic hue, shoot sparks of faith and love that burn away the breath of darkness. Oh, Lady Sharka, it is a dying sigh of life to last in blackness as the flames go out.'

For a moment, Sharka was captivated by his confusing words. It was as though he had been transformed by the sight of the black stones that the old woman threw down, as though they conjured some magic in his mind only accessible on rare occasions of insight or enlightenment.

Sharka shivered. She shook herself, as if breaking free from the attentions of an unwanted lover.

'So, what do you see, old woman? What is shown in these stones you throw before me?'

'I see blood, cold blood.'

'I can see that any time I wish. What does your vision mean?'

'I see the cold blood of death. So much of it. It runs like a river. It flows down a broad channel into a place of light. There it brings its contamination, its darkness. It poisons the world with its infection. It has been held back by death, but the dam that has restrained it will fail. It may be driven back temporarily, but in the end it will be irresistible. In the end there will be no power strong enough to hold it back, and then the coldness it brings will last forever. And I see more. I see a trail of light—'

'This is nonsense! Do you take favours like gypsies for your stupid predictions? Perhaps you should tell me how many children I will have and what will be the colour of their hair!'

'I say only what I see, my lady.'

'Then you see nothing I do not know, hag.'

'Madam, there is nothing to know; there is only the fact of it. I do not tell you what I know, I only tell you what is. Mistress Sharka, you are on a precipice. Your future lies below you like an abyss. Lady Sharka, your blood is mingled—goodness and evil are combined within you. As your blood is mixed, so your soul is joined with another. Act before your blood is cold. It is already too late to bring the life of the carrier of the shadows to an end. The carrier's life is endless.'

'What do you mean, it is already too late?'

'I mean you are destined to follow a path which goes beyond the path set for you by another.'

'Then my own path leads me out of here.'

'Lady, after every one who visits, another passes through the world. It is a constant flow of souls, a constant pattern of occurrence. The world has no other colours and no other temperature. Like ice, if it is not cold, it does not exist, and, like the world, in the absence of the sun, everything is darkness—there are no shadows in a world of only shadows. Act now on your own accord, lady, or your future actions will seal your fate forever.'

'Dagan! Take us out of this place! Take us away from this madness!' Sharka climbed up onto her horse and, still adjusting her feet in her stirrups, she bent to Jewel and

Julian. 'I spare your lives only because I do not have the time to kill you.'

She rode away quickly. Her newly formed band followed closely behind, and behind them ran a small group of heavily loaded servants she had chosen for menial tasks.

A year later they arrived at a foreign port. It was at the furthest extent of the kingdom—they had travelled to the outermost edges of the wilderness, seen what was there and were now ready to return to Atho.

Sharka stood on the quayside, fighting with her fear of the water below. Her hair spun out from the back of her neck like sea-spray. She turned into the warm breeze and smiled. She was perfection. She looked as if she had arisen from the pearly lips of an opening shell and been borne to the earth as an example of all the gods had decreed as good and beautiful.

Dagan stared at her from the other end of the harbour wall. He worshipped her—her muscular strength, her tallness, her flowing, tangled hair, her bare taut thighs. Her existence completed his world—it always had ever since the first moment he had been brought to her by Treasure. He winced as her bangles flashed in the hot sun. For him she was a glittering form too much to behold—he was a simple mortal and her presence was too ethereal to bear.

The sight of her transported him into another world. He no longer saw what was before him. Instead he saw himself standing back fearfully as she strode across his path, and barred his progress. He sat at her feet as she squatted by the campfire. His heart quickened as, with the increasing coldness, she draped her heavy furs across her square shoulders. Dagan longed to caress them—the furs her servants packed on mules each day, the furs she wore daily in the colder northern climate into which they had travelled, the furs that decked her out as a glacial animal with a frozen heart. Each day he glanced against them inadvertently and shivered with the thrill of it. He imagined their contact against her skin as she pulled them up around her neck to shield her from the chill of the darkening nights. He imagined her body heat contained between their filaments, her naked skin brushed by their delicate strands.

How he wished to be her shining knight, strutting across the steppes of the outer wildness in her service against an unconquerable foe, going forward to his doom knowing that his life had not been in vain and that she would provide purpose for its sacrifice. How he wished she would lead him into her castle—a prisoner of desire. He swooned as he saw himself following her into the darkness. He cringed in nervous anticipation as he felt her fearless energy. He thrilled at the thought of her caprice and changeable mood. He imagined how she had toyed with him and played with him until suddenly, for no reason at all, she became bored with her toy and had him stretched on a wheel until his body broke. The thought of that exquisite pain, of suffering the random outcome of her will, made spit dribble over his bottom lip. He could not help his embarrassment as he thought of being reduced to such imbecility, but he could not prevent it. He thought of how, later, she would call him "Sannyasi", a term of endearment he had invented for himself when he imagined her at his feet. He pictured her curled up before him submissively, warming her limbs by a massive fire of logs.

'Sannyasi, my master,' he heard her purr. But it was ridiculous. How could she serve him? He would get down to her and crouch even lower, knowing that she was only humouring him with a moment's madness. Of course he was not her master, he was "Ctivad", her slave, and he felt the pain of humiliation as, on all fours, he bent low and kissed her toes one by one. Then again she turned on him, and kicked him into the fire and he was set alight and burnt as a sacrifice to his love for her.

Suddenly, he felt the sun on his face—the heat was real. His daydream was ended. Sharka stood before him in the warmth. She turned away from the coppery sea. Her hair blew across her face. She ran across the rope-strewn quay

112

towards him. She looked like the young girl he had sat down in the back of the church in Atho and wide eyed had stared up at him as he told her tales of adventure and brigandry.

'Dagan! What do you think of this place? Should we settle here? You could teach me to swim. Yes, even that! I could sit astride your shoulders and you could grasp my ankles. Dagan, is it possible?'

'No, mistress, it is not.'

His heart broke as he spoke; it was as if she had burst living out of his dream, offering them a new life together and he had turned it down. What sense of duty drove him to such idiocy? He could not imagine; but it did.

'You are right, as always, Dagan. Fantasies like that are for the weak minded and purposeless. We must return. We will sleep here on the quay then tomorrow we start for Atho.'

The next morning was the start of a beautiful summer's day. They rode quickly inland. A cock's crow cut slices from the air, and the humming of early-morning insects filled in the gaps that were carved out. Sharka was filled with an overwhelming sense of purpose. As she rode towards a distant tower, she felt her life unfolding before her—it was as if she had been reborn. Her skin prickled with the energy and excitement that poured in heavy waves through her pounding veins.

They travelled by day through endless forests and paced their journey by the regularity of the stepping-stones that punctuated their passage—the castles like islands in a sea of green within whose safe walls they slept at night.

On the way, Sharka had exchanged one of her ageing servants for a fresh horse—a chestnut stallion—with a down-at-heel noble they had shared a rest stop with. Dagan remembered the servant, leaving when the deal had been done—looking back like an abandoned dog and cowering under the blows of his new master. Later, they had heard from a runner going south, that the same noble had died of bee stings and gangrene and that the servant had stolen his horse. Dagan saw the look in Sharka's eye that signalled her intention to find the erstwhile servant if ever they should return, kill him and recover the horse, or if the animal was dead then claim any reward that may be on offer for the servant's body. When she spoke, she said exactly that.

Sometimes, she spoke to Dagan with great tenderness, wishing the best for him, and expressing deep concern for his welfare. Sometimes she dismissed him angrily as if he were a hindrance.

'Yes, even you old friend, tire me sometimes,' she said as she turned to her faithful band after striking him unwarrantedly with her whip—their eyes already on her, waiting for her instructions—and told them all to go to sleep.

They rode for several days beside a sluggish stream. Where it slowed into murky pools it reeked. Beside one of these pools they came across a young man and girl. Sharka held back and watched them. Each pushed playfully at the other as they laughed. Everything each said was a source of amusement to the other—their company produced boundless joy to each. She watched as the young man removed the girl's blouse and ran his hands around her firm youthful breasts. He pinched her nipples and she rose up against the tender pain, closing her eyes and licking her lips in anticipation of the something as yet unknown

The pair was startled when Sharka and her men rode up. The girl tried to cover herself but she fumbled with her shirt and it fell into the smelly pond of black water.

'What makes you so happy?' demanded Sharka.

The girl's face flushed red as she held her arm across her small breasts in an attempt to cover her nipples.

'I do not know, mistress,' she said. 'We are just happy.'

'What are you saying to each other that makes you laugh so?'

'He is funny, mistress. But he is gentle as well. Do you not laugh like us when you are in the company of your lover?'

114

'No. I only have one lover and I have not met him yet.'

'But when you do, will you not be amused by him, mistress?'

'No. I will treat him like this.'

Sharka removed her sword from its scabbard, held it above the girl and slashed it deeply into her neck. It penetrated her chest and cleaved her apart. The young man sat up wide-eyed and panic stricken. He went to grab the girl but saw it was pointless. Instead, he jumped to his feet and ran away screaming. Sharka pursued him and cut off his head.

That night Sharka had the young man's head impaled on a spike and the men had to sleep beneath it.

'Get used to the sight of your future,' she told them. 'Sleeping beneath that which draws you on will imprint your own fate into your mind.'

Several days later, they came over the crest of a low hill and a wide plain opened up before them. Next to an isolated copse of trees stood a small castle, little more than a manor house. Its white painted walls glistened in the sun and, from the roof of a squat tower, a tattered red flag waved lazily in the warm breeze.

'Where is this Dagan?'

'I think it is Timisoara Castle lady.'

'Whose is it?'

'I do not know. I am not sure it is that castle even.'

'Dagan, you are failing me.'

There was the glistening sparkle of a tear in his eye.

'I would never fail you mistress, never. My faithfulness to you is never in doubt.'

Sharka threw back her mane of hair, and rode at full gallop towards the safety of the castle gates. She wandered around the castle walls all night subjecting the guards to questioning or testing them in ways that Treasure had taught her in order to ascertain if any of them were members of the flock or in any way tainted by Luit's hand. When the sun

115

arose she ordered Dagan to wake the others so that they could depart and continue their search elsewhere.

Another time they approached a castle called Savara. The route was winding and slow and they saw the castle for three days until finally they arrived at the last rocky crest that stood before it. She ordered her men to stop and she stood on the rocky outcrop to survey the scene before her. Her large fur bonnet rested low on her high forehead and her breath condensed around her in the cold early morning air. She crinkled up her eyes and smiled; she looked like a mischievous dragon. The white painted pentagonal mass of the castle seemed like a vain attempt to camouflage its austere and overpowering bulk with a superficial purity. She rode into the castle with her men straining to keep up. She entered through the open gates and slaughtered all she could find. Finally, Dagan lifted her exhausted and covered in blood and flesh from her horse, helped her to a pile of corn bags and straw where she dropped down sweating and breathing in sharp ecstatic gasps.

'Dagan, were any of those our enemies?'

'I do not think so, madam.'

'Does it matter that I have killed them?'

'No, my lady, it was your decision and in your hands.'

'Then it was right.'

'Yes, mistress, it was right.'

'Dagan, you are my rock.'

11. Faedra

The rain in Athala, soaking and heavy even when Luit broke through the conduit for the first time, had over the years become ever worse. Now it was continuous—grey and foreboding, it filled the air, the ground had become a marsh; there was no escape from it. The occasional breaks that brought with them the musical dripping from the branches of trees had ceased; now the only sound was the constant drumming of the continual downpour. The latest deluge had not let up for many months, mould had formed on living things, and moss covered the trees in puffy green cancers. Even as it rained, clouds descended to the ground and covered everything with a drenching mist. The rain fell from within it, as though it had no source or becoming. The flock had taken to sheltering permanently in isolated places beneath trees or overhanging cliffs. They had stopped moving about, stopped seeking the light of beacons, stopped seeking food and feeding. Many were too ill to move. Luit visited them but they were not pleased to see him. They stared at him through milky vacuous eyes, slowly following him as he moved amongst them like an unwelcome phantom come to witness their terrible immortality for his own pleasure.

Out of habit, he fed the beacons and lit any that were put out by the incessant inundation, but even as he did it, he realised the pointlessness of it all. His hands were sore from the work, the skin had softened more than usual from the constant exposure to the unrelenting rain and now it came away in clumps from the bone and muscle beneath. It did not bleed so much, but the mould that was everywhere got into the open wounds and spread an infection throughout his body that caused him constant nausea. The burden of his life, the sickness of the flock and his isolation from Atho had caused his fears to turn darker than at most times he could cope with. He dreaded waking and facing another day of wandering in the rain, of witnessing the terrible product of

117

what at one time had seemed the perfect answer to a life cut short by untimely death. The idea of sleep only foretold of increasing misery as he saw the next period of wakefulness entering his consciousness through wearied painful eyes.

One day, as he trudged to an extinguished beacon, he found one of the last newcomers to be brought through the conduit by Lezma huddled beneath a fallen branch. She was pale and shivering with cold and fear, but unlike the other inhabitants her body was well fed and rounded.

'Why are you alone?' he barked.

'I have been rejected by the rest,' she said shakily. 'I am not the same as them. It was a mistake to bring me. I have not been able to taste the sweetness of immortality. I wish to go home but there is no one to take me. I fear I must die here, and I am too young.'

'If you have not tasted the sweetness of immortality, then you are lucky.'

'How can you say that, master? It is everything we all want. To live forever—surely nothing can be more wished for?'

'You have been saved from the greatest evil that can be bestowed on a living thing. As you shiver here, bemoaning your loss, you are in grace—the grace of a known death, the kindest grace of fate, the grace of annihilation.'

'You cannot say that, master. All in Atho hope to be chosen to come, all wish for the day that your messenger appears. They wait for her at the gates. They stand in lines hoping to be chosen. Tears fall from the eyes of those left behind as she escorts those selected to your promised land.'

'Then they are mistaken in their hopes and wishes. They stand in line in the hope of horror. This promised land has lost its flavour, it is a prison where only the suffering come to be punished.'

'You cannot mean that, sire. I would wish more than anything to be young forever, to feel the vitality of youth, to always have the appetites that course only in the early years of mortals. I would wish more than anything to know that only eternity was before me. Sire, I cannot face the idea of dying—it is more than I can stand.'

'You are a stupid girl. What is your name?'

'Faedra, sire.'

'What does that mean?'

'It means "bright", sire. I was named this because I was born as the sun rose over the sea of Atho.'

'Stand up, Faedra! I will give you a taste of immortality.'

She stood up shakily and wiped rain from her eyes and cheeks.

He took her hand and led her towards the trunk of a massive dripping oak. She shied away at first from the pulpy feel of his soapy skin, and the strong rotting flavour of his scent, but she submitted to his strength and presence and only with the slightest resistance followed him obediently.

'I do not mean to pull away, master. It is being so close to you, being so close to eternity, which makes me fearful.'

He heard movement in the sopping undergrowth and turned. For a moment he thought it was Lezma. He thought he saw the golden flash of her peachy skin. A thrill ran through him, a sudden burst of energy rippled in his veins. For a moment he felt again the worth of life, the point of being. For a moment he sensed again the value of a never-ending future. He tried to penetrate the rain with his stare. If it was only her, he would lift her high above his head, throw her up and catch her, spin her in his hands, clasp her close and promise her anything—if only it was her.

Two time-worn bodies emerged from the bushes, their grey skin taut on their skulls, their hands trembling as they clutched each other in a confused mixture of fear and need.

Luit hissed at them. They tightened their grip on each other but did not have the strength to pull back; they no longer had the energy to express their fear in any way other than trembling.

'How many are there of you? Come out! Come into the presence of your lord!'

Another appeared, wide-eyed and bent, and then another holding onto a crooked stick for support. Three more crawled into the open on their hands and knees without even looking up.

Luit stood and watched as the rest of the flock slowly emerged. Some managed to stand, others lay down as soon as they could drag themselves no further, some supported each other, some held onto branches or sticks. All shook with the cold and damp, all were grey and soaked, all were hungry; their staring eyes bore testament only to a deeply embedded and utter hopelessness.

The sight of them appalled Luit. They embodied all his failed hopes. He saw in their eyes and their trembling bodies his own shattered dreams.

'Master?' one of them mumbled weakly. 'Is there hope?'

Luit crinkled up his eyes. The saltiness of his tears burned the raw edges of his eyelids. He thought again of Lezma—of the possibility of hope. A flash of it drifted through his mind. The idea that all was not lost filtered through the misery of it all and for a brief moment he saw again why it had all seemed worthwhile.

He pushed Faedra's face forward against the heavy rough tree trunk. Some of the flock that lay on the wet ground crawled forward.

'Look! I have some new blood for us! She is willing to share it! It will give us new vitality, new life! You must not give up hope! Yes! I say to you, there is hope!'

He reached down to one of the flock—an emaciated woman with only one arm. A rough grey rope was pulled round her waist so that when she could not walk others could pull her. Luit tore it from her. She spun as he ripped it away and she fell to the ground, fearfully thrashing the stump of her missing arm in the brown greasy mud. One of the others pulled her to her feet but she stood quivering with anxiety now that her lifeline had been taken from her.

Luit bound one end of the rope around one of Faedra's wrists, extended it around the tree and bound the other end tightly to her other wrist. Her face was pressed sideways against the coarse bark. She gasped in shock at the suddenness of his attack and her eyes widened with the realisation of her predicament.

'Master! Master!' she shouted. 'I will obey you willingly. There is no need to bind me!'

He ignored her pleas, pressed her hard against the tree trunk, grabbed her skimpy wet smock at the shoulders and tore it down to her waist.

'Look! See the colour of her skin, see its plumpness, see the veins on her neck, and see how she pants at the thought of being so close to her master. Listen! Hear how she cries out my name! Listen to her desperation, her need for fulfilment, her need to be part of us! She wants so much what we have.'

'Please, master! It is painful!'

Faedra pulled at the ropes that held her, but the rough bark of the oak tree scored at the skin of her breasts and cut into her nipples. Blood trickled down from the scratches and ran underneath her armpits and onto her waist. It mixed with the rain and its colour diluted into a slimy translucent pink.

Luit tore the smock further, exposing Faedra's plump and rounded buttocks and the tops of her thighs.

'See how shapely she is! Look at the curve of her waist, the fullness of her buttocks, and the crack at their centre. See how she squirms with excitement at exposing her body to you. See how she wriggles at the thought of your attention. She senses immortality. Come closer. Closer!'

One of the flock, resting heavily on a gnarled stick, moved forward and touched Faedra's buttocks. He breathed in deeply as the feel of her skin reminded him of his passions, of the foundation of his desire for everlastingness. He touched it again—yes, it was still there, the need to live, the anticipation of the delights life could offer. He ran his fingers along her crack and felt at their tips the softness of her fleshy cunt. Its moisture clung to his skin and he picked up a waft of its delightful scent in his half clogged nostrils.

Luit could see the refreshment the touch of her cunt brought to the wretched man.

'Yes! This is what we are here for! To enjoy the sensations of life forever. All of you! Come! Feel the flesh of this vital girl! Touch the worth of immortality! Sniff at her moisture! Inhale the fragrance of promise!'

Another crept forward but when he reached out he immediately pulled back, afraid of what he might discover, afraid that he might find only disappointment and that his already bleak world would turn even darker. Luit saw the fear on the old man's worn out face. He saw the abysmal blackness that surrounded him. He saw its impenetrability. The others sensed the old man's disappointment and fear as well and held back, unable to fight the foundation of their inertia and respond to their master's call.

Luit looked at them all—his flock! His heart sank. The promises of eternity had come to this! He was filled with a desperate anxiety—undirected, painful and bursting to escape.

He undid his broad leather belt and dropped his coarsely woven trousers to his knees. His bulging penis stood out, throbbing and heavy. He thrust his hands between Faedra's thighs. She shrieked. He parted them roughly and exposed the darkness of her anus and beyond that the half hidden pinkness of her fleshy cunt. His desperate frustration overwhelmed him. The beckoning sight of her flesh filled him with desire—at last, a longing! He stared at her. He anticipated the joy he could feel from her and without any pause drove himself into the next moment of his experience.

Rain poured down on them as he forced his heavy penis into her tight virgin anus. She cried out in pain as, squeezing the muscular ring wider than ever before, it began to enter. It was unyielding at the entrance and his glans was pinched tightly as it entered. But each time he pulled back, the rain poured down his shaft and lubricated it so that he could force it further in. With every thrust he felt her tightening on it, squeezing herself around it, trying to hold it back. But her resistance only inflamed his need for more. Her eyes widened, spit ran from her mouth and she pressed the side of her face against the rough oak trunk in anguished horror. The pain against her cheeks distracted her only momentarily from the pain of her filling rectum.

It was as if she was being stuffed to her throat. She felt as if she was suffocating as she coughed and choked. His scent filled her nostrils and she shivered with cold as all the time he pushed harder and deeper. She screamed again and heard the sound of her cries mixing with the pouring rain in a throaty babbling gurgle. She could not hear her own voice in it—it was as if she had become disembodied and foreign even to herself.

The strain was great for him. His heart pumped heavily and his body ached with the effort. He gasped loudly as he penetrated her ever deeper with his burgeoning penis. She squirmed wildly and the tightness her movements provided again filled him with a surge of need. He held his penis inside her rectum. She cried out in agony.

'Come closer!' he shouted to the flock. 'See the pleasures of life! Watch your master penetrating the flesh of another!'

They tried to move forward, but still weakness and exhaustion dominated their abilities and his encouragements were hollow. They stood or lay where they were, staring vacuously—rain sodden and deaf to his entreaties to taste again the delights of life.

Luit was angered by their weakness. He had brought them here to serve him, to be his companions for eternity. He had given them the gift of everlasting life and they repaid him only with lack of will and resentment.

He thrust his penis deeper into Faedra's anus until it would go no further. He felt it throbbing against the constriction, beating heavily in her innards. Through it he felt her gasping breaths, her heartbeat, the pulsing of her blood. He closed his eyes, fleetingly picturing Lezma in his mind. If only! He dropped his mouth against Faedra's neck and bit into it hard. He felt the thick muscular wall of her blood vessel between his teeth as he closed them sharply together.

Blood spurted from the punctured artery. He reared back, cried out with joy then buried his face again against the splashing flow of bright red blood.

The flock murmured—a vague excitement rising in them from the site of the crimson plume that spurted from Faedra's punctured blood vessel. Some of them sniffed at the air but the rain was so hard nothing of the aroma of blood could travel through it. Even so, the sight of it reminded them of their need, of their hunger, of their dreadful permanency in life.

He sucked at the blood but it wasn't to his taste—he needed venous blood, blood without oxygen, blood that was hungry for his own infection. He bit deeper into her neck again, gnawing at it roughly, spitting out chunks of her flesh until he severed a vein and its darker blood flowed freely into his mouth.

It poured across her shoulder and down her back. He was inflamed by it. He thrust his penis wildly inside her rectum as he supped hungrily from the gaping wound. He paused for a moment and looked back at the flock, letting them see his blood-smeared face, the skin and severed vein that hung from his mouth, the joy of it all. He urged them forward with his stare, willing them to rush and join him, to take part in the feast, but he could see they were too weak, too despaired, too resigned to the blackening misery that had consumed them. With one last thrust his ardour was concluded and with it his hopes. He held his pulsating penis deeply inside her as his semen ran freely. It ran from him in long slow surges and filled her up with its heat.

He breathed heavily, filling his lungs again with the

cloying wetness of Athala; as his body recovered from the strain, so his mind recovered from the temporary light of optimism that had broken through the shadowless abyss of his eternal darkness.

He withdrew his throbbing penis from Faedra's anus. His semen still pulsed from its end and flowed down the insides of her thighs. Her head had dropped to the side and her face was scratched and bleeding where it had rubbed against the rough bark of the tree. He drank one last time from the stream of blood flowing from her neck. He glared at the flock, untied the rope that secured Faedra to the tree, flung her over his shoulder and walked away with her into the now torrential rain.

He worked his way slowly through the forest and back to the entrance to the conduit. He rested Faedra on some ferns that were almost dry beneath a thickly leaved spreading bush. Semen still ran down the insides of her thighs. He placed a stone on the puncture in her artery and bound it tightly with a leather cord to stop the flow of blood. He used his surgical skills to repair the wounds he had caused to her neck, for some of the work using parts of his own skin he peeled away with a knife. Her anus was torn and he sewed that with a needle and some thread he made from his own hair. Every few hours he released the pressure on the stone at her neck so that her blood flow did not congeal and become infected. When she was conscious, he fed her on berries and let her drink his own blood.

He watched over her most nights, bathing her scratched face and running his fingers through her bloodstained hair. Three times again he saw the fleeting glint of a form moving quickly amongst the bushes. He knew it was Lezma—he could smell her lemony fragrance, and he could sense her capriciousness as she ran through the woods spying on him, tantalizing him, shadowing him with her glitter. He knew she was jealous of the attention he was giving to Faedra, and he continued doing it knowing that it would hold Lezma's attention and keep her close by. As he checked the stitches in Faedra's anus, or when he changed the stone bound into her severed artery, he felt the pleasure of Lezma's stare, the heat of her pent up jealousy. When he caught a glimpse of her shape passing between the sopping trees, or even thought he heard her pushing through the leaves, his heart pounded heavily as he thought again of her entrancing company and enthusiasm.

After some weeks Faedra recovered enough to stand. She had lost her youthful plumpness and was beautiful and athletic. She walked naked in the woods collecting berries and fruit and he prepared a bowl of blood for her to drink each evening when she returned.

'Faedra, I want you to go to Atho for me. The flock is desperate for replenishment. You have seen how weakened they are. They cannot survive without fresh stock.'

'I will do anything for you, master. Tell me what it is.'

'You will go into this dark entrance, into the conduit, and find your way to Atho. There you will collect as many as you can find and lead them back.'

'How can I do that master? I do not know the way. Surely it is impossible?'

'There is one that knows the pathway—Lezma, my fallen elf. She will lead you. This is how. Unknown to her, I will cover her feet with a substance that glows in the dark. You must follow this glowing light until she leads you to the exit on the Atho side. I will give you some of the substance to carry and, as you journey behind Lezma, you can mark out your way so that it will be easy for you to return.'

Faedra nodded slowly.

'Will this make me immortal, master?'

He saw the look of hope and expectation in her eyes.

'Perhaps, who can tell?'

She sat at his feet and drank some blood from the bowl he held out for her. Later that night, as she slept, Luit turned over many stones and found handfuls of the black scorpions that exuded the luminous lime green light. He placed half of them in a bag and the rest he crushed and wiped on a bundle of fern leaves. He spread the leaves carefully at the entrance to the conduit.

He gave the bag of scorpions to Faedra and they both waited near the entrance until one evening, just as the murky sun was disappearing, they saw a glinting form flashing from the darkness of the conduit. It was Lezma. She had walked over his trap and her illuminated feet could be clearly seen dancing quickly in a circle at the entrance. She cartwheeled twice then skipped back into the darkness. Faedra did as she had been told and followed.

Faedra kept as close as she could without being noticed. Lezma's feet flashed through the blackness like fireflies. Sometimes she skipped, sometimes pranced, once she even cartwheeled as she sprang from a small pool she had to swim across. Faedra always kept her in sight. Even when Lezma swam through the large pond at the conduit's centre Faedra unfailingly kept track of her. At every turn she took one of the scorpions from the bag Luit had given her and smashed it against the rock wall. Straightaway it lit up and glowed leaving a trail that upon her return she would easily be able to follow.

Eventually Lezma squeezed through the little portal she used above the main exit on the Atho side. As soon as she was out of the dark the lime green light on her feet disappeared. When she was sure it was safe she walked down to the city and slipped in through one of the gates along with a band of entertainers that already had permission to enter. Faedra waited until Lezma had run all the way down the hillside and was within a short distance of the city walls before she emerged.

Lezma spent that night with the entertainers around a fire they built behind a storehouse in the main square. They were accomplished acrobats and storytellers and she joined in with her own acrobatics. They formed a pyramid and she clambered to the top to everyone's delight and much applause. One of the stories they told was of a great bell made from the most precious metal on earth—a platinum bell. It was the greatest of weapons and could defeat any population by making them insane. They said it had been cast in a mould that had taken ten years to form and that after it had been polished and tuned it had never been sounded. The only defence was to plug your ears with wax. After the stories and the acrobatics they all slept together and for the first time in her life Lezma felt comforted by a sense of belonging drawn from the close company of others.

12. Beyond the dead pile

Sharka sent a messenger ahead to warn of their return to Atho. Treasure was pleased to receive the news and organised the citizens to line each side of the road to the city gates in readiness. Most held banners or garlands of flowers and some held the forks, spades or rakes they used in their daily work. The naked young girls who attended Treasure in the church carried bowls of the last flower petals that could be found and threw them down in multicoloured showers in front of Sharka and her retinue when finally they appeared.

It was a triumphal entry, as if Sharka had won a new kingdom or defeated a long resistant enemy. She dismounted in front of the church and was greeted like a returning hero by Treasure. Dagan walked behind her; proud of his association with her homecoming and the accolade she was being given.

From the walls hung a wicker cage suspended from a rope attached to a timber built gantry. Inside it was Faedra, clawing at the willow bars, scowling, spitting and stamping her feet on the woven base of her swaying prison.

Treasure kissed Sharka on both cheeks and clasped her tightly in both arms.

'They are cheering you because they believe you can save them. They are desperate. They have captured that child you see in the cage in the hope that her suffering will save them. She said she was from Athala and had come to take more back to its master. They did not trust her because she was not the usual emissary. They did not know how she had found her way here. The men raped her and threw her into the cage in the hope that Graf will take her as a sacrifice. They will swing the cage out over the walls as it gets dark. She is the second they have captured and treated like this. The first they found hiding amongst a group of entertainers. Someone recognised her as the messenger Luit himself had sent here. They beat her with flails, drove her naked through the streets, poured honey over her and then imprisoned her in the cage. Graf took her in the dead of the night three days ago and the next morning a healthy deer was seen running on the hillside. They hope this second one will bring another good sign.'

Sharka looked up at the captured girl.

'What is your name?'

'Faedra, mistress.'

'Where are you from?'

'Athala.'

'How did you find your way here?'

'By the light, mistress. I just followed the light. My lord Luit showed me how. You could do the same. You could find the master by the same light. Release me, mistress, and I will show you the smudges of light.'

Sharka stared at her hard. She remembered Jewel's words: "follow the trail of light that is smudged in the darkness"—she shivered as they came back clearly into her mind.

Treasure held Sharka's hand and led her away from the cheering crowds and into the church. They sat behind the heavy curtain that was stretched at the back of the ornate altar.

'From what do the citizens think I can save them?' asked Sharka.

'A pestilence has broken out.'

'We have seen signs of it in the wilderness. Crops are dying and the fields are barren in places.'

'Yes, but it has become worse. Now it is taking the lives of the citizens. They do not know how to deal with it and are filled with fear. They say you will be their salvation. They have been waiting only for your return. I can do nothing for them; I am too old and weak. My darling Sharka, at last it is your time.'

'What do you mean?'

'After all these years of preparation it is time for you to fulfil your destiny, it is time for you to carry out the deed for which you have been preparing since I first took you into my care. You can save these poor souls, yes, but you must attack the source. And that is where you will achieve the goal of your life. Attack and destroy the source. That must be the only thing in your mind from now on.'

'Have I time to rest?'

'For a few nights, yes, then you must act.'

Sharka lay down where she was and went straight to sleep.

Dagan moved over and sat close to her.

Treasure knelt down in front of him.

'Is your mistress ready for the trial that awaits her?'

'Yes, she is.'

'Does she have a faithful band of followers who will carry out all her orders?'

'Yes.'

'Have they been trained in dispatching the flock?'

'Yes.'

'And you, will you do everything in your power to help your mistress achieve her goal?'

'Yes, I will.'

'I am pleased. Now, there is one more thing. There is something you must do for me. Sharka is my agent; you know that, you have shared her training with me since she was first brought to Atho. Now it is her testing time. She must not fail. If she does then Atho is finished, the evil of Luit and his kingdom in Athala will leach into our city and pollute everything. She must not fail.'

'I understand.'

'We all have times of weakness, even your mistress. I fear now that I cut short her training and she may not have sufficient commitment to carry out her task.'

'My mistress is as firm as any. Surely she will not fail you.'

'She must not. Take this and administer it to your mistress.'

'What is it?'

'A poison.'

131

Dagan jumped up angrily.

'What are you asking me? What nonsense is this?'

'Be calm. It is not nonsense. It is a slow acting poison, it will take many months to do its job, and there is an antidote—a complete and sufficient antidote.'

'Why should I give it to my mistress?'

'Because she needs to know she must succeed. The antidote will be sent to her when she sends the message that her task has been successfully concluded—that the evil Luit is finished.'

'Why should she falter? Why should you mistrust her so?'

'I do not mistrust her, but she may be under his power, she may need to be reminded of her only true imperative. You must not underrate Luit's strength and his desire to remain forever in this world. Dagan, can you do it?'

Dagan looked into Treasure's eyes. He knew she shared with him a devotion to Sharka that stretched back to her very beginnings in Atho. He could not let his mistress fail to complete what had been intended for her all her life. He could see no option. His fate in this was sealed and yet still an uncertainty flowed within him—how could he willingly put his mistress' life at risk?

He looked down.

'Remember your oath, Dagan? Remember swearing that you would fulfil my future wish when it was requested?'

'I do.'

'And so you guarantee that your three younger sisters will be safe.'

'What do you mean?'

'They have been testing out the poison for me. They are already feeling its effects. My young girls tell me that they are all beginning to vomit each day. It is not much— they think they have eaten something rotten—and it will take a while before it becomes worse, but worse it will surely become. I must be sure to get them the antidote as well. I must not forget because I am worried that you will not fulfil

132

your promise to me. I must not forget, must I, Dagan?'

His uncertainty passed—his options closed.

'No. Give it to me. I will do your bidding.'

With a heavy heart he ordered the band of followers to gather around their leader and sleep. They did not question his order, feeling safer in her close company even when she was not aware of their existence.

The next morning she rose early and went around kicking them all to wake them. Dagan brought her already saddled horse and before it was light they rode out of the city. They passed beneath the now empty cage that hung from the gantry over the walls and followed the course of the river that led up into the hills.

The river stank, and its stench got worse as they came closer to its source. The once pure fount of water that nourished Atho had become a septic trail of black and nauseous fluid. Sharka's men covered their mouths and noses with cloths to try and protect themselves but it was impossible, the evil in the smell was too powerful to be kept back by such primitive means. One of the servants fainted and had to be carried by the others. Sharka did not cover her face.

They stopped for two days and rested. Sharka lay against her sleeping horse and meditated. She told Dagan that sleeping close to the scent would acclimatise them and make them stronger.

Early on the third day they arrived at the massive wall of bodies built slavishly by Graf. He was not in attendance; he had wandered to the city's burying place in the night and had located two recently buried bodies. He was waiting again until darkness came before removing them and bringing them back to his macabre project.

Sharka rode across the front of the dead pile—it was like a cliff: its overhanging projections the limbs and heads of bodies forced into its face to plug any holes, its vegetation the rags of clothing hanging from the corpses stuffed carefully into its wall. But its height was so great and the weight of stinking water behind it so forceful, that it could not entirely hold back the pressure. Many places on the face seeped and from its base, the black water of Athala's river leached out like tar into Atho's sun. The stench was unbearable. Several of Sharka's men vomited and two of the horses they rode reared back and could not be controlled.

'What is the purpose of this, Dagan?'

'It is a nightmare come into the waking world, mistress. A cliff of the dead.'

'Why is it here?'

'I do not know, lady. It is a work of evil.'

'Is it the source of the pestilence?'

'No, I think it is what it is holding back which is the cause. The black tar that seeps from the base of this disgusting pile of flesh is what runs into Atho. That is surely what has caused the pestilence.'

'But where does it come from, Dagan? All waters arise. Something at its origin must be the source of the germ that these foul waters bring? We are only seeing the outflow here, not what has created the evil contained in the blackness which runs from this terrible dam.'

'Of course, mistress. It comes from your destiny. It comes from where we must go.'

'Yes, I feel it! At last, I have found the purpose of my life! Beneath this towering mass of horror I have come to my fate. Dagan! Bring these weaklings that follow me forward! Look how they cower. Are these the warriors who have pledged themselves to me? Are these the fighters who will accompany me to my destiny? Bring them forward! Set them to work!' I am sick of their feebleness!

Dagan rounded up the men, cajoling them and kicking at them as they pulled back time after time from the wretched stinking pile of rotting corpses.

Sharka jumped down from her horse and grabbed a pallid gangrenous leg that hung near the base of the pile. She pulled it free and held it in both hands like she would her own sword. She railed at her men, striking them with the severed leg, wiping it across their hose, reaching up and pressing it into their horrified faces.

'Serve me or leave! You show the faintness of your hearts at the first obstacle. Leave if you are too weak to follow! Leave!'

She ran amongst them setting their horses into a panic, kicking at them, swinging the rotten leg around her head with such force that when it struck one of her men who was holding up his hands in horror it knocked him cleanly from his saddle to the ground. She placed her foot on his chest.

'I offered you revenge for the branding of your ancestors, and you repay me with cowardice. You are no better than one of Treasure's servant girls. Here! Take this limb! Take it! Climb up the wall of this rotting dam and plug the seepage that runs from its face. Here! Take it! Take it or go back to the wilderness and tell tales of your weakness!'

There was a moment's hesitation—a time of measuring one evil against another, a moment of weighing one future against a worse, an interval when the anticipation of regrets is set against their absence. Suddenly, the man grabbed the leg and scrambled up the wall of bodies until he reached the obvious leakage in its face. He stuffed it in the gap keenly, the stench, the revulsion, the horror of it all driven out of his mind by a compunction to lead his life fully, to meet his own death with a feeling of worth, to live up to the oath he had pledged to his unyielding mistress.

Another ran forward and picked up a head that had rolled from the pile; one of its eyes was hanging out of the socket on a white and pink striated cord. He plunged the head into a small fissure that issued stinking black water. The eye hung down unseeingly on its thread. He reached out and tore it free. Staring straight at Sharka, he stuffed it in his mouth and swallowed it whole. His action inspired the others. Another followed and they all joined together, picking up dislodged parts of bodies, looking for leaks in the wall and plugging them as well as they could. Some emulated their comrade and broke off pieces of the remains and consumed them, sucked at them, or wiped them across their faces as if cleaning themselves with their stinking slime.

Soon all the seeps and trickles in the pile had been staunched. Only the tarry leak from its base continued to run. Sharka's men brought more limbs and pressed them into any gaps they could see that might be letting the black water flow, but it would not stop—the pressure of the river in the conduit was too great and the weight of bodies in the wall too immense to allow anything to be pushed beneath it. When they tried, the rotting edifice rocked unnervingly, its deathly bricks slithering against each other as its foundation was interfered with and threatened to give way.

'We have done enough here. Put props against it. It will hold well enough until we return.'

They gathered some timber props and shored up the wall of corpses. Suddenly one of the men cried out.

'A movement! Mistress, a movement!'

All eyes turned to where he was pointing. A hand twitched then waved from half way up the terrible pile. It sagged, the effort was so much, then it tried again—a pathetic wave, a pitiful signal.

'Use the props! Climb up and see what it is that lives amongst this stinking pile. See what it is that can survive amidst so much death!'

The men built a precarious ramp from the timber posts. Supported by the others, one of them climbed up but he could not reach the hand. Another climbed up and struggled onto the first one's shoulders. He rocked from side to side as he reached as high as he could. In the end he touched the hand. The waving suddenly became frantic— incensed by contact with another, enervated by contact with a possible rescuer. He touched it again and it grabbed him, knocking him off balance. He fell from the shoulders of the first man and he in turn fell from the supporting props. The hand did not let go and, as the men toppled to the ground,

136

Lezma was dragged out of the wall and fell in a tarry, slime covered heap on top of them.

A sudden burst of black water was released from where she had been. The men struggled to build the props again and worked to plug the gap she had left. For a while it seemed impossible but in the end the stream was staunched.

Lezma lay on the ground gasping for breath. Her frail body was bruised and blackened, her eyes sunken, her face pale and drawn. Her smooth skin dripped with filthy black tar.

'Who are you?' demanded Sharka.

'Lezma. I am Lezma. I am an elf, I am...'

She stopped and gasped for breath. She rolled on her side and vomited.

'Who placed you here?'

'Graf. He took me from the cage the citizens placed me in days ago...'

'Tell me more!'

'I watched him running up to the walls in the night. He climbed up and shook the cage, then tore open the wicker bars and dragged me out. He is very strong. He was enraged when I told him I was Luit's servant and could help him find favour with my master. He was so angry. I thought he would kill me. He tied me to a rope and dragged me behind him beneath this rotting pile for a day before climbing up and wedging me into its stinking face. I have licked honey from my hands to keep myself alive. He was so angry. He was—'

'I don't trust you. You will remain here until we return. If your captor finds you first then he can do with you what he wants.'

'If you are going to Athala, I can lead you through the conduit.'

'Why would I need you to lead me?'

'Because I know the way. Inside it is all darkness. No light will shine inside the conduit.'

'How would we enter? The entrance is blocked with this wall of corpses.'

'I have my own entrance. Look! Higher up the hillside. See that tussock of moss. Beneath it you will find another way in. It is tight though, you will have to—'

'Tie her up! She stays!'

They tied Lezma to a post and drove it into the ground at the foot of the dead pile. They turned her face to watch it so that she would be there to greet them on their return.

They released the horses, climbed up the hillside above the dead pile and found Lezma's entrance.

'You will not find your way through! Only I know the route to Athala,' she shouted from below.

'You are not Sharka. There is no route barred to me.'

Sharka had her men make torches. They stood in a line waiting to enter. She thrust her torch in first and immediately it was extinguished—the air would not sustain it. She tried another but it was the same.

'We will go into the darkness!' she cried.

They threw their torches down and, one by one, with Sharka in the lead, they entered the conduit beneath the tussock of moss. Some of the servants held back but eventually they were induced to go in. The last but one was just squeezing in as Lezma released her hands—they had not tied her well. By the time the last man's head disappeared beneath the mossy mound, Lezma had already freed her legs.

Inside the conduit, Sharka crouched down waiting for her eyes to become accustomed to the darkness. The flashing lights that spun in front of her vision passed, but they were replaced only with intense blackness. Her men crouched behind her fearful and silent—dependent upon her actions, and her ability to decide upon which of them to take. Sharka looked around thinking again of Faedra's words. Suddenly she saw a flicker of light. She rubbed her eyes thinking it was only the dying flashes of the light outside scratched onto the backs of her eyeballs. She looked and again saw the flicker—a lime green flash illuminating nothing more than itself. Sharka moved towards it slowly. She hit her head hard on the low roof. She remained motionless for a moment then continued feeling her way towards the light. Sensing her movement, her men followed behind. She touched the lime green source when she reached it and straightaway saw another, apparently further in the distance.

'Follow the light!' she called back to them. 'Follow the light!'

She tracked each flash of light, slowly clawing her way through the inky darkness. When they came to the first pool she told Dagan she could not go on. She sat at its edge trembling with fear.

'I am finished. It is impossible for me. The touch of water tells me my mission is at an end.'

'You must go on,' he said. 'Your life depends on it. Nothing must stand in the way of your mission. Nothing!'

She tried to step into the unseen water, but she could not. She fell to her knees and cried. Dagan cried with her. He knew she could not retreat but her fear barred the way to any progress as surely as if it was a massive timber drawbridge.

They slept in the darkness unable to proceed. Dagan wanted to help her but could think of no solution. The men were unsettled by their leader's uncertainty and fear. Sharka stood all night against a cold rock, dozing every now and again, dreaming fleetingly, jumping when she realised she had just woken from a sleep she did not even know she was having.

'I will not be stopped!' she shouted.

Dagan jumped up. The men fumbled in the blackness for something to tell them where they were. Her voice echoed into the labyrinth.

'I will not be stopped. You will carry me. You will bear me above the water. I will entrust myself to your hands. Your certainty will be my guarantee. It is all I ask. Now, bind me so that I do not lose faith and struggle against you. And make it tight so that I cannot move anything of my arms, my hands, my legs, or my feet. And gag my mouth tightly before you bind my head to the handle of a sword so that I cannot shout out or turn my head. Do it!'

They used her own sword, laying the blade down her back with the large two-handed hilt behind her head. They used laces and belts to fix her head to it and a leather belt to gag her mouth. She submitted silently as, in the darkness, they bound her arms to her sides and her legs together. It was difficult work in the dark and they checked their slow progress by feeling all of their work as they proceeded. When they were satisfied, they tied her to two more swords they laid at her sides. Eventually, she was completely immobilized.

On Dagan's order, they lifted her above their heads and waded into the pond. The stench was overpowering. Most of them had made masks to help protect them from the worst, but the beneficial effect was small and most of them coughed and choked as the vapour's reeking sting entered their throats. They did not know how deep the pond would be and when the water level reached their necks they swam. It was hard to keep Sharka clear of the water but they used all their strength until finally, exhausted and disorientated, they reached the other side. They undid the gag and started to release her.

'Keep me like this!' she shouted. 'There will surely be more water. I will be under your control until we reach the exit. Check my bindings are fast! My fear erupts within me even as I speak and I cannot hold it back. Bind me fast! If I shake myself free and fall into the water then I am surely lost. And gag me tightly so that I cannot issue any different instructions.'

They did as she ordered and dragged her or carried her as the height and constriction of the passageways dictated. It took an hour to swim the deepest pond at the conduit's centre and several hours to recover their strength enough to carry on when they finally reached the opposite shore. All the while Dagan followed the lime green flashes on the walls or roofs. They faded sometimes, and some had been so hurriedly made that they were only the slightest prick of light. But it was enough and, as if it had never been in question, they suddenly found themselves emerging from the conduit into the murk and rain of Athala.

The men fell to the ground, gasping for breath and struggling to focus their eyes even in the dim murky light that greeted them. Sharka lay bound to the swords, staring up into the cloudy sky, waiting for her release.

Carefully they undid her bonds. As she was set free, she shivered with the aftershocks of her dread. She had contained the stress of her fears for the whole journey and now her body, exhausted by its constrained anxiety and tension, released the enforced inhibition in fitful jerking shivers. Dagan rubbed her shoulders in an effort to ease the strain but she shrugged him off angrily.

As they sheltered beneath a nearby overhanging rock, Lezma peered out of the entrance and watched them excitedly. She pursed her lips and frowned then ran forward, cartwheeling through a small clearing before disappearing in the silver sheen of Athala's torrential and remorseless rain.

13. Sharka in Athala

Strings of lichen hung from sodden branches—their colours barely discernable in the half light of the cloud filled sky—worms and slugs, the only moving life, brought a slimy creeping glitter to the saturated world. In Athala, the rain no longer cleansed—it smeared everything with the grease of decay and encouraged only decomposition; it starved everything of air and threatened everything with the fear of suffocation or drowning.

Sharka hung back beneath the overhanging rock, afraid to go out into the rain. She looked about nervously; everywhere there was a sense of foreboding, as if the earth itself had become infected with something putrid. But she was not afraid of that, indeed the very sense of evil incited her to move forward, it was the rain itself that fell from the sky that froze her to the spot and prohibited her from further action.

'We will wait here,' she said. 'Dagan, come to my side, I feel ill.'

'What is it, mistress?'

'I feel pains in my stomach. I have a deep sense of nausea. Dagan, I feel as if I might die before my mission is complete.'

'It is only the rain, mistress, and the tension of the journey here. You are fighting with your fears. The anxious strain is a suffering to the body.'

'Dagan, I cannot face this rain and I know of no solution.' She clutched her stomach and folded up in pain. 'There it is again. It is such a fierce pain. It is like a creature inside me, a rat gnawing away at me, eating me from the inside.

Dagan looked worried. He knew the poison must be working inside her. He knew it was a critical point in his life, and he did not want to face it.

'We must not fail, mistress. Your life has been devoted to this time. There must be a way. There must be a way of going forward.'

'Leave me to think. You are right, we cannot be stopped now. Leave me.'

All night the rain hammered around the entrance to the conduit. All the men clustered together with the servants beneath an improvised shelter they had cut from branches and ferns. Sharka watched them huddling together, seeking safety in the closeness of each other's bodies, waiting for her to act, their lives committed to the devotion of being in her service.

As the dim light broke and the rain kept pouring, she ordered them to cut four long poles and build a square shelter fixed at their tops so that she could walk beneath it as they supported it at each corner. They set about their task busily and soon constructed the device according to her plans. They carried it to the conduit entrance and stood ready to escort her beneath it.

She stepped out into its shelter. Some drips of rain fell through the fern covering which was its roof but it was dry enough. She ran her fingers through her hair and stepped forward. Her four escorts walked forward in time with her and she remained beneath the protective canopy, safe in their hands, protected from her fear, and the rain that fell from the sky in a continual heavy downpour.

They came to a clearing. For the first time she saw the object of her mission—Luit! He stood on the edge of the small rain soaked area that formed a circular dell amongst the heavy trees.

The thickness and noise of the rain was so great that Sharka and her men were able to move quite close without being seen or heard. Sharka stood beneath her canopy, her heart beating fast, her eyes fixed on Luit.

He had gathered all the flock together, walking around the whole kingdom, and rounded up individuals, pairs and small groups that had become spread throughout the land. Some of them had not seen him for many years, some had forgotten that there were others; all suffered from

143

the same fateful neuroses and fears that led them to a hopeless abandonment of their own welfare and any will they had for a meaningful future. He had driven posts into the ground in the clearing and woven a corral of wicker into them. He had herded all the flock in there, tethering them if he thought they had the strength to escape each time he left them and set off again to bring back others. Now he had them all. They stood shivering and soaked, those that could stand clinging onto each other, those that could not, lying on the cold muddy ground.

He entered the corral and stood in their midst—his long hair hung on his shoulders, his rain soaked face pale and disfigured, his hands and arms bare and covered in mutilating scars and disfigurements.

'I have sent an emissary to Atho. I expect her to return soon with fresh blood. You have been deprived of an adequate source for too long but the problem will be remedied. Do not lose faith in our compact with eternity. The fruits of our everlastingness will be bountiful and filled with joy. But this cannot be without sacrifices. I have decided that while we wait for our new members we will nourish ourselves from within our own number.'

He reached down to a woman who was lying at his feet.

'This poor wretch will sacrifice herself for the rest of you. See, her eyes are alight with the prospect.'

He pulled her up by the neck. She barely had the strength to cough as his fingers tightened around her throat. He shook her in an effort to make her seem more alive. Her eyes wandered from side to side—she could not respond and he dropped her back to the ground.

Sharka watched as he selected another. He poked her eyeballs, pressing his fingertips against them until they dished in under the strain. But this one could not react either; her exhaustion with living had overwhelmed everything about her and existence no longer had any aim. Luit pulled his fingers away and shook his head. A trickle of pale blood ran from one of the woman's eyeballs where his broken yellow nail had punctured it. He licked the end of his finger. The blood had hardly any taste. He sucked at it and spat it out onto the muddy soil. One of the flock near his feet managed to move enough to lick at the blood-soaked saliva he had spat out. She ran her tongue into it and scooped it up slowly before taking it into her mouth and laboriously swallowing it.

'See!' he shouted. 'It is nourishing her! See how the lust for life comes back into this hungry one! We can feed on each other! We can satisfy our need with our own blood. Here. I will puncture another one. Sup from the wound, feel your life being filled again with zest!'

He stabbed his fingernail into the woman's other eyeball. It seeped a mixture of blood and grey humour. It ran down her staring hopeless face—she no longer cared about pain; her body was meaningless to her. He licked her cheeks to encourage the others to feed, but none could summon up the will to follow his lead. He dropped the woman to the ground. He looked around the flock and was filled with dark despair.

Sharka stepped forward, the four men carrying her canopy moved with her. She announced herself.

'I am here because of your emissary, Faedra! I am here in response to your call for more to join your flock!'

For a moment Luit was confused; he was not accustomed to the voice of another and was surprised by its suddenness and clarity. He looked towards it source and saw Sharka, standing beneath the canopy held by her men.

'I have followed the trail of light and have brought you new stock,' she called to him. 'Look at them, see their strength. I am Sharka, your salvation.'

Her long wet and tangled straw-coloured hair stuck to her high forehead and cheeks. Her broad mouth, edged by her full lips, held open expectantly. Her piercing blue eyes cut through the silver sheen of pouring rain. Everything about her transfixed him. It was as if he had seen an

145

apparition. She took a step forward, her men kept pace with her, sheltering her from the storm and from her fears. Luit saw how gracefully she moved—her long legs, her lithe figure perfectly in control, no hint of hesitancy, nothing other than a body committed to purpose. He tried to step towards her but found himself glued to the spot. He tried to call out but his throat had dried and he could not utter a sound. He stared vacuously towards her, lost in her bright blue eyes, pounded by the gale of hope and desire which from nowhere she had suddenly brought to him.

'Can you not speak? Have I travelled here to meet someone who cannot greet me?'

'Yes...I can. Who are you? Are you a dream?'

'I am no dream. I am Sharka. Receive me.'

'Have your men lead you to the shelter of the trees. Here, tell them to bring you here.'

Sharka walked beneath her canopy, her heart beating wildly in her chest, her mission at last nearing completion.

Luit knelt before her.

'You are so beautiful. You have filled my heart with a yearning I thought was lost to me.'

'It is right that you kneel. Desire should be viewed from a lower place. The beloved should always stand above the one who loves.'

'Tell me again. Are you real or are you an apparition? I cannot trust what I am feeling.'

'I am real.'

'Then I thank any gods who may exist for gracing me with you. Have you come to stay?'

'For as long as I need. I must refresh myself with sleep. I need to have my clothes dried. My men must be instructed in their new duties.'

Two of her servants came forward and began unbuckling her waistcoat. Her white shirt was wet and her prominent dark pink nipples pressed hard against the translucent linen. The servants peeled her waistcoat away and unbuttoned her shirt. Her small breasts and slender body

146

shone with moisture. They removed her sword from its scabbard but left her leather belt firmly fixed at her narrow waist. They peeled down her tight hose. She stood, completely exposed, her hose wrinkled up at the top of her leather boots, the rest of her body naked and glistening.

'You may touch me if you like.'

Luit's heart throbbed at the forthrightness of the invitation. He could not resist—her offer was like an instruction he could only obey.

He reached out his pulpy hand and ran it across her naked angular hips. He drew the backs of his yellow cracked fingernails across her tight flat stomach. He let them slip into the top of her delectable, precise and naked crack. She did not move as he slipped his finger along the delicate furrow of her flesh. A gleam of moisture appeared along the slit. He held his finger to his nostrils and inhaled deeply. His mind was filled with all he desired—a cloud of want consumed him. The prospect of immortality had started to glow again within him; in that delightful scent he had found again the spot in time when he had first discovered his longing for life. Everything within him that he had tired of was at once refreshed.

Sharka's servants removed her hose and boots. She stood beneath the canopy wearing only her belt and empty scabbard as her men built a shelter between two heavy tree branches that hung like cradles from opposing oaks a distance away. When it was finished she was escorted to it and she lay down on a large pillow of ferns they had placed in the driest part. As she parted her thighs the pink gleam of her crack drew Luit's gaze like the warm glow of nectar would draw a bee.

He followed her and lay beside her. She did not in any way resist him but remained aloof as he explored her body with his fingers and kissed her with his desiccated lips. Her disinterest only excited him more. When he probed his tongue into her mouth and tasted her sweet saliva he was more excited by her distracted impartiality than by the

147

intimacy of his contact with her. When he parted her thighs and exposed her gleaming cunt, he was thrilled more by her detachment than by her willingness to allow him to do anything he wished to her.

Unable to hold back, he mounted her, drove his throbbing penis into her, and rode upon her as he would a horse. He gasped as his penis entered and he howled and grunted as he fought to maintain a tempo in his ardour. She did not buck or shy away from him but neither did she respond to his entreaties for more pace or passion. She could see in his bloodshot eyes and hear in his panting gasps that simply allowing him to indulge himself within her body was in itself an overwhelming and almost unbearable pleasure for him.

His ailing body was soon exhausted and he fell from her wheezing and gasping for breath. His body was slow to recover but she took his softened penis into her mouth and soon he was able again to fulfil his need for further orgasm.

She stayed with him for three nights. Each night was the same: he proclaimed his love for her, penetrated her, rode her and filled her with his semen. On the second night he vomited explosively from the exertion of it all. After this, the stink of his body increased and some strips of ill matching skin that he had only recently sewn to his hips came undone. On the third night he felt the need to subjugate her, to place her at the mercy of his will, to punish her, to make her scream with the pain of delight, and he threw her forward on all fours and delivered several blows to her upturned buttocks with his leather belt. But still she did not show any sign of succumbing to passion; she remained aloof and even with red welt marks across her taut buttocks did not make him feel that in any way he possessed her.

Every morning Sharka suffered pains in her stomach. She had completely lost her appetite and looked very pale.

As the third night was coming to a close, and Luit was sleeping fitfully, Dagan dropped down on his knee beside her.

148

'The mission is pressing, mistress. The men are tired of the rain and they have not eaten properly since we left Atho.'

'Nor have I.'

'It is not good for you, mistress. We should act. Perhaps we have waited long enough?'

'Are you questioning me, Dagan?'

'I am reminding you, mistress, that you have a mission and that you must not be distracted. It is essential you are not distracted.'

'That is not a clear answer, Dagan. Why are you not speaking plainly to me? Have you become a philosopher?'

'I am concerned for you, mistress, as always. This time I am especially concerned for you.'

'Why?'

'Because you are ailing, mistress.'

'It is a stomach cramp, nothing more. It is my night time exertions!'

'But it gets worse the longer we delay. If you would act then perhaps it could be remedied.'

'Perhaps I should not carry out my mission? Perhaps this man needs me more than I need to carry out what has been planned for me. Perhaps it is time to free myself from the slavery of my upbringing?'

'You cannot, mistress! It is impossible! You cannot think that! No, mistress!'

'Dagan! You have never spoken to me like this before.'

'You have never faltered before, mistress.'

'Are you taking me for a coward?'

'Of course not. But the mission is essential. If you do not carry it out then—'

'Then what? Speak! This sounds like a threat! Dagan what are you saying?'

'I can hardly bear to say it, mistress—'

'Speak!'

'You must act. If you do not you will die. There I

have said it—'

'We will all die, Dagan. This is foolishness.'

'No. Mistress, if you do not act then you cannot be saved from...'

She cradled his chin in her hand. His heart was pounding.

'Cannot be saved from...from what? From what, Dagan?'

'From your faithful servant, mistress. You have been poisoned. You have been poisoned by Treasure months ago. It is a slow acting poison. When the mission is carried out then I will send word for her to dispatch the antidote. Mistress, how can I say such a thing to you?'

There was a pause—only the sound of rain.

'Dagan! How could you take part in this?'

'My family have been poisoned too, mistress. I know it is weak of me. I did not know what to do. You know I am faithful to you. You know none thinks more of you than me. I cannot bear to think you will die from this terrible act. I never doubted for a moment that you would not carry out the deed you have been trained all your life to complete.'

'Dagan, you need not have doubted me. My dedication was never in question. No poison was necessary.' She craned her neck and whispered to him. 'Do your part now. Be as silent as possible. I do not want my moment disturbed by distraction. Slay the wretched flock in the way we have agreed. They will only die finally when I have completed my mission. You need not have doubted me, dearest Dagan. I have not faltered.'

He shivered with excitement as her warm breath passed against his ear. He nodded and went back to the others.

She could just see through the rain as he gathered her men together. She felt a strange wave of tenderness sweeping through her—a recognition of their faith, their service and her power over them. It was as if they were part of her life's fulfilment and she was enhanced by their being.

150

She watched them arming themselves—testing the weight of their swords, picking up the stakes they had prepared days before by sharpening them at each end, looking at each other in acknowledgment of their mutual actions. She watched them surrounding the corral where the flock were still herded and she knew that in their actions her fate was at last unfolding.

14. Sharka acts

Sharka's men stood around the corral, each taking a position equidistant from those on their right and left. Every one of them held his sword in one hand and a heavy mallet in the other. They had carried the long stakes to the side of the corral and propped them in stooks like sheaves of wheat. The flock looked dazed and hopeless. Those that could stand walked in slow meaningless circles—some holding hands, some clutching the ragged clothes of those they followed, some watching their feet as if their own pointless paces were something to follow. Those that lay on the soaking muddy ground reached up their hands and clawed weakly at the rain as though trying to draw it into their throats and drown themselves.

Sharka's men looked to Dagan for instructions—they knew that their leader had her own mission but that each of their efforts would have a combined effect. Dagan watched the pitiful ambling of their quarry, deciding when their final tragic moments should be brought to an end. He wondered about the value of a few extra seconds in respect of eternity. A strange image of it flashed into his mind—a solitary figure, suspended in space, facing nothingness. It seemed senseless to continue with their misery—there was no gain to be found—the blackness of annihilation was their only future; there was no one moment better than any other when the darkness should begin. These hapless creatures were prisoners of their own weakness and victims of their own misplaced hopes. He allowed a short pause—time only to inhale—then climbed over the weak wicker barrier and stepped amongst them.

They murmured and pushed against him as if he was their saviour, and for a moment he felt like their redeemer; he wanted to sweep them up and lead them to salvation away from their futile misery and the incessant rain.

A woman knelt at his feet. She clasped her hands together and turned her pale drawn face upwards.

152

'Mercy, lord,' she said weakly.

He nodded to the men and took the first slice—bringing his sword down at an angle against the neck of the pitiful kneeling woman. The blade severed her neck and her head rolled to the ground, leaving her body still kneeling and her hands still clasped together in prayer. The ends of the main arteries on either side of her neck issued blood but her heart was so weak and her pulse so feeble that it simply ran away down each of her shoulders with only the vaguest hint that its flow was being driven by a living heart.

The other men lifted their swords and this single murder became carnage.

Treasure had told them that if necessary the flock could be subdued by dazzling them with torches—the brightness would confuse them and send them into disarray, she had said. But it was unnecessary—there was no resistance, no will to persist in life, no strength left in them. The men sliced their swords across the throats of those that stood or lay. Their heads fell like toppling balls or rolled aside on the muddy ground. The blood, the glazed expressions on the faces of the toppled heads, and the sloppy thudding sound they made as they hit the mud, caused alarm in those whose turn for death had not yet come. The wearisome apathy found one last burst of energy. The flock cried out together as a wave of panic spread through them, then in horrified unison as they saw the flashing blades cutting through the air and bringing their doom. But the slaughter was rapid and merciless and their final howling could do nothing to stem it and was short lived. Their faces contorted, their mouths opened wide and their tongues flickered and lapped as their heads were sheared from their bodies. And when they fell in the mud, or rolled against a clump of moss, their mouths continued moving, their tongues continued lapping, and their eyes continued blinking. Several of the decapitated heads spoke, somehow using the air in their mouths and the last vestige of muscular power in their faces to form words. One said, "Thank you", another, "I forgive you", another asked, "Is this the end?".

Sharka's men rammed the spikes that had been sharpened at each end into the ground. They gathered the heads and thrust them neck down onto the roughly carved points. Some of them bit the men who carried them—one sinking its teeth deeply into the man's wrist and making it bleed copiously. When all the heads were in place, the men took the mallets they carried and hit the tops of the heads until they were driven firmly onto the sharpened stakes.

Now, as if stimulated by the terrible punishment, more of the heads found a voice. Several of them screamed, several blubbered, one cried out for salvation, one swore an oath of vengeance. Some sang a hymn, one spat and cursed, some cried out their names as if that would somehow guarantee them identity in an un-witnessed future. The men twisted the heads on the spikes, trying to stop the cries and screams, trying to bring their slaughter to a close, but it was an hour before the dirge finally quietened to anything like enough to tolerate without the welling nervousness of anxiety that it bred.

The men sat huddled together surrounded by the heads. They clung to each other fearful of what they had done, unprepared for the outcome of their actions and unable to protect themselves against it. Some stared down at the ground, some stared at each other hoping for affirmation that he had acted rightly. One of them jumped when one of the mouths moved again or one of the bodies tried to crawl and repossess its dismembered part. The longer they sat, the more animated the headless bodies became. One of the bodies crawled over the men's legs and none of the men was able to move as it made its way unseeingly over them. Each man watched in frozen fear as the body pulled its way forward on its elbows, grasping their legs or clothing, dragging its weight across them then dropping to the ground and continuing with its journey. The body crawled to one of the spikes, pulled itself up on it and tugged at the head in an effort to free it. The head opened its mouth in an effort to speak but could only form a silent gaping yawn. The stake toppled and the head came free. The body's hands grabbed it and held it above its shoulders. It tried desperately to place it against its severed neck but it was weak and clumsy and dropped the head to the ground. The head spoke in an effort to guide the body's actions but the body crawled away in the wrong direction leaving the head pleading with it to return but knowing it could not hear or respond.

The men's anxiety was increased by concern that Sharka had not shown herself. But they knew what they had to do next. With trembling hands they replaced the fallen head on its spike. They pushed wicks and tapers soaked in oil up the nostrils, in the ears and into the mouths of the heads and set fire to them all. They paced the corral anxiously walking amongst the bodies in the spluttering light the burning heads provided. Still some of the heads spoke, even as the flames consumed their lips and burned their tongues, even as their ears were in flames and the cavities of their nostrils filled with fire, they managed to utter their own names or cry out to the bodies that still crawled around in the mud. In panic at their unstoppable movements, the men pulled away or slashed their swords randomly across the bodies as they clutched at the men's legs or reached up to grasp their clothing. The men severed the bodies' arms and legs and chopped their torsos into pieces. They cut out their genitals and hauled out their viscera, but still the body parts moved or crawled and the organs that had been cut out throbbed or pulsated. In the end the men climbed over the corral fence and watched the pieces of bodies, swiping them away if any of them came too near the edge of the corral.

Dagan went to each one of the men and put his arm around his shoulder.

'You have done well,' he said to them in turn. 'It is a hard task but a right one. Now we wait, and then it will end.'

Close by, Luit slept in Sharka's arms. She looked down at pieces of his tattered skin flickering red in the light of the fires that filled the corral. But she did not see

155

disfigurement and rot; she saw only the handsome image captured in the icon she had slept beneath for most of her life. She saw his vigour and optimism, she saw the hope he held for his future and the pride he felt in his achievements. She had watched him each night of her life in Atho. It was as if he was her father—he was imprinted on her mind.

She ran her fingers across his forehead. She wondered if he would wake, if he would need to thrust her again, if he would need to feel the rush of his semen as he held his throbbing penis deep inside her cunt. She pinched his skin, hoping that he would wake for just one last time, but he was exhausted and could not be roused. A piece of his skin dislodged. She looked at it quizzically—as if it captured all that he was. She tasted it and spat it out.

Her dagger lay beside an uneaten apple. She picked it up and without a moment's hesitation she drove it deeply into his heart.

He opened his eyes in shock and looked at her. He knew she had stabbed him. He did not care, he thought it an act of passion, an expression of her desire and he felt his penis hardening under the pressure of his own response to her assumed ardour. But he saw in her dispassionate face no sign of passion—just the oblique stare that he had witnessed throughout all his ardour. She twisted the blade. He felt it inside his heart. Again he looked for desire in her face but saw none. She twisted the blade again. There was a pain but it was dull—years of self-mortification had blunted his awareness of hurt. He felt it cut the carcass of his heart; he felt the sharp edge of the blade slicing through it. He felt it bleeding inside his body—some blood simply leaking, some being pumped out under the full pressure of his damaged heart. He coughed and tasted the blood in his lungs. She drove the blade deeper, pressing the hilt into his pulpy skin and causing it to break away in a messy tear. Then, from somewhere inside his flesh, he realised that he would die.

The realisation surged through him in a massive tide. He would die! At last he knew he would die! His eternity was over! At last the only hand that could steal his immortality had struck. But how could this be so? How could the object of all his passion be the child who could wield the hand of death? No, it was impossible, but he felt life leaching from him, he felt death's darkness encroaching. There was no mistaking it!

Sharka watched him, inquisitive to see his life ebb away, curious to see the conclusion to her lifelong task. She did not smile or gloat, but she knew that at last she had attained her goal. She picked up the apple and looked at it, wondering where to bite into it next.

He spoke calmly.

'Sweet Sharka, my sweetest beloved, why have you done this?'

'My whole life has been directed to it.'

She turned the apple in her hand and bit into it.

'And so mine, Sharka, although I did not know it. My endlessness has haunted me and yet all the time it was my destiny to die. My dearest, you are the bringer of my fate.'

'Each of us lives our own fate. It comes no matter which road we take. I bring this apple's fate in just the same way that I bring yours.'

'But how can it...?' He half closed his eyes as the recognition of what was happening swept over him. The backs of his eyelids brightened as if they had been set on fire. 'Can it truly be?'

'It is as it was predicted. It is as it has happened.'

Luit looked into her crystal bright blue eyes and saw the answer. They were the eyes of the child he had dispatched in Lezma's arms those many years ago, the child he had commanded Lezma to destroy! She was the only one who could end his eternity, the only one who could bring him peace. She was his only child, the only hand that could bring his death. He thought of questioning her, of trying to solve the puzzle, but he knew it was pointless—he had no interest in it, the moment of his death pressed harder on him than the need to resolve what now seemed the mere trivia of life.

'I am sad to leave you, my dearest, sweetest Sharka. I have only just found you, and now I must leave you, and that is indeed a sad thing. And, after all these years of waiting, I am not ready to go. After all the time I have spent wishing for an end, now that it is here I cannot bear the thought of it. But it is only because I cannot abide the thought of leaving you. How cruel it is that when I find the only reason I have to exist, it is that very thing which takes it from me.'

'An end comes to us all, even those who think they have cheated it. While we live, we touch death. While we are awake, we touch sleep. While we hope, our fate is already sealed. It is all confusion. My dagger has dispatched you, and my intention has driven it into your heart. But I have not killed you. A greater power has taken you. It is the power of what is to be which now steals you from life, from what you thought it would be. You are being taken away, and soon the same thief will take me also. Perhaps we will be together when he gathers us all and places us in his cave? Perhaps we will dance together and throw our reflections on the wall so that others can be confused by our nature. I shall look forward to it for then we will be at a higher stage than we are now. At least we will be closer to the shadows that presently deceive us.'

'But to have only just found you, my sweet.'

'We have exchanged our passion, but you are the victim of my life's mission. I have been hunting you since I have known anything. I have been training to kill you and you did not know it. You need not have been so haunted by the prospect of eternity, for it was never going to be. There is no more to it. Now you will die.'

'My end is at your hand, my dearest, at your hand, and there is no more perfect place. As death darkens my eyes I can see the perfection of it all. You have grown into the perfect child, and have been the perfect lover, and you have dispatched me with a perfect stroke of your loving hand. How I have wished for this moment. So long it has evaded me and you, my treasure, have brought it as your sweetest gift. With this single cut you have brought me my freedom at last. I cannot bear to leave you, but now I can see that leaving you is the greatest gift you could bring me.'

'It is so,' she said as she cradled his head in her hands and took another bite from the apple.

'But the cost is not only my life.'

'What else can it be?'

'There is a new knowledge that transcends my death.'

'I know no more than I know.'

'But you are the living proof of my knowledge. Your own life will provide testimony to what I now know. I have learned the greatest secret of my life with my last breath.'

He dropped his head back. She shook it, anxious to know what he meant. His soft skin broke between her fingers. What had he meant? What was this testimony he had provided? His grey eyes quickly glazed over. She pressed her fingers against his forehead—the damp coldness of true death already on its glassy surface. For a moment she wished she could shake him back to life and demand an answer. She drew her dagger from his chest and wiped the blood from its blade on his dirty shirt. She shivered and closed his eyes by running her fingers down across his lids. She took a final bite from the apple and tossed the core down onto the muddy ground.

As the apple hit the ground the final twitches on the last charred faces of the flock stopped. Luit's energy had gone. His flock spoke no more, their bodies became still. At last, with their master's departure, they were allowed to rest in the final, complete and welcome darkness of death.

She let go of Luit's head and held her stomach. Luit's body fell crumpled to the ground, his face turned to the side, blood seeping from his open mouth.

Sharka had her men cut up Luit's body. She started eating a fresh apple as she watched them; it was hard for her to swallow and when she did manage to get it down it made her feel nauseous. The men severed Luit's head, arms and legs and cut off his genitals. Two of them brought some burning logs they had been using for a fire overnight, threw the genitals into a pan and fried them. They offered the sweetmeat first to Sharka. She held it up by the penis and sucked at one of the testicles. She bit off a portion of the fried meat and swallowed in a hungry gulp. She passed it on to the men and each of them took a share.

After they had eaten, one of them slit open Luit's chest and removed his lungs, another cut a wide cross in his stomach and removed his liver and kidneys. They fried the kidneys and liver but this time, although the men all ate their share, Sharka declined and continued to eat her apple. One of them, wiping his mouth, pulled out Luit's stomach and intestines and set fire to them. Inhaling the acrid fumes from the burning viscera, they hung every part left and the remaining carcass from the low branch of a massive tree. Rain mixed with the blood that ran from the remains and dripped onto the muddy ground. Sharka said that any man who wished could drink some of the blood and rain that oozed down. It would both refresh them and finalise their feast. No one hung back and each in turn knelt beneath the parts and drank fully of the blood. Dagan collected some in a bowl and brought it to Sharka. She emptied it on one draught but as it entered her stomach another wave of nausea filled her.

'Our task is complete,' she proclaimed. 'You have done your duty well. You have taken your revenge, and I have fulfilled the aim of my life. Now we must find our way back to Atho.'

She dropped to the ground clutching her stomach, writhing in an agony of pain and vomiting explosively into the brown greasy mud. The men sensed the urgency of her instruction but were filled with fear as they saw their mistress—their leader, the only one who looked after them—unable to control her body and unable to service them with the strength they needed from her.

An apprehensive pause followed. The sound of the rain faded into the background as the retching sound of Sharka's vomiting became the only thing to be heard. A sudden burst of light broke through the heavy clouds and disappeared as quickly as it came. Suddenly, a flickering naked form dashed between the sopping bushes.

Sharka coughed and inhaled a mixture of mud and vomit as she gasped for air. Lezma cartwheeled towards the corral. She giggled, jumped over the wicker fence and pranced between the body parts. She touched one of the heads. It was still hot and she pulled her fingers back shocked. Dropping her head from side to side, she looked at each of the charred heads on the spikes. Some of them still burned, their sizzling fat dripping down the spike upon which they were secured in white bubbling streams. She poked her fingers into the mouth of one of them and mimicked an imaginary voice as she forced the jaw up and down in a ghastly mime. She danced between the severed sliced up bodies, poking at them with her toes and every few steps bending quickly and licking blood from their wounds. She spun around and dropped to the ground. She rolled amongst them and covered herself in their blood and viscera. She howled and hooted with excitement then rolled forward in a tight ball, bouncing against the bodies or tipping to one side and another.

Covered in mud, blood and the gluey remains of body tissue and entrails, she climbed back over the fence and danced in circles around the perimeter of the corral. She wiped the rain down her body, bathing and cleaning herself. After she had completed three circuits she ran to where Sharka was sitting and dropped down by her side gasping for breath. She pressed herself closely against Sharka then abruptly sat back with her legs crossed, her back straight and her hands placed on the tops of her knees.

'So he is dead. At last, your father is dead,' she said still gasping.

Sharka looked at Lezma and doubled over with a

161

sudden cramp of pain in her stomach.

Sharka recovered herself and inhaled deeply.

'What do you mean?'

'What I say, mistress. I can repeat it for you, if you like. "So he is dead. At last, your father is dead". I have a good memory do you not think? I remember everything. Ask me something and I can give you the answer. Let me see, yes, your last question was "What do you mean?" and my answer was—'

'My father is dead? What do you mean?'

'Mistress, have you forgotten you have asked me that already? Perhaps you need a memory elf like me to help you remember things. Mistress, I mean what I say. I am Lezma, look I am as fiery as a dragon and so quick you would think I had wings. Watch me run and jump. Sometimes I leap over the moon. Let me breathe fire for you, mistress. Hold out your hands and your little dragon will warm them with her breath. Perhaps you would like me to serve you? But perhaps I could not. I think I have had enough of service. He is dead! Look! Your father is dead! Oh dear, my poor master is dead.'

Sharka grabbed her by the neck.

'Tell me what you mean!'

'Mistress, I mean what I say.'

'Then say it again.'

'Your father is dead. Hold out your hands and let me warm them, they are so cold. Are you unwell? I can see sweat on your forehead.'

Sharka dropped her to the ground. Lezma jumped up straightaway and started gambolling in circles.

'Tell me!' shouted Sharka.

'Of course, he is not my master any more. I had enough of his orders: "do this", "do that", "Lezma come here", "Lezma go there", "Lezma turn cartwheels for me". He never wanted you anyway. He gave you to me. Look, you have aged and I have not! I am immune from aging. It is because I am an elf, or because I am a dragon. I do not really know why. Look at my body. It is like it was when he first found me. I think he was jealous that I stayed perfect when all the time he had to keep repairing himself.'

'Tell me more. Tell me your story.'

Sharka doubled over with another sudden stomach cramp.

'I can remember it perfectly because I am a memory elf. I took you through the conduit. I ran like a flash. Like the wind! Whoosh! I wanted to get back to him. He thought I was only thinking of the boys, but he was wrong. He told me to stab you with a spike and leave you to die. He gave me a little hammer and a spike. I still have the hammer. What a father! But you had a trinket at your neck. It was so pretty. I had to have it. He never allowed me anything! And he banished me for that! What a cruel father he was. But *I* didn't get any older. Look I am as young as the youngest fairy! Hold your hands out. They are so cold. Let me blow on them and warm them up.'

'This is nonsense. How can I be dead when I am alive?'

'Because I did not carry out his orders. I saved you. Yes, I am your saviour.'

'This is foolish. How can this be?'

'It can be because it is. I can prove it.'

'Then do so,'

'If you expose your naked legs you will see the wounds that I made when I drove the spike through your shins. And on your hips you will see the bite marks I made. I sucked your blood. It was so sweet. I can taste it now! Look at my teeth! Let me show you how they fit the imprints in your skin! Perhaps you would let me open up the wound again?'

Lezma danced around Sharka, baring her teeth and cartwheeling in frantic excited bounds.

Sharka stood up and pulled her hose down to the tops of her leather boots—beads of sweat glistened on her forehead and her cheeks were wet. She looked at the scars on her lower legs—exactly as Lezma had described. She had never known what had caused them.

Lezma ran forward and knelt at Sharka's feet. She lifted her face against Sharka's hip and pressed her teeth into the wound in Sharka's skin.

'Look how my teeth fit into the marks in your hips! They are perfect. This is how I did it. Look, I will bite into them again and you will feel it as you did then.'

Sharka kicked her away.

She needed no further proof of the story. She swayed to one side and fell to the ground, clutching her stomach, filled with pain and nausea and overwhelmed with the tragedy of what she now realised was her terrible act—she had taken her own father as her lover then slain him.

15. The messenger

Dagan chose a man to go through the conduit and pass the message to Treasure that Sharka's mission had been accomplished. He was a strong and proud man and had been the first to come forward when Sharka had asked for volunteers from the descendents of the banished in Oskia. He said that he would count the mission as the greatest honour of his life. Dagan gave him precise instructions. He made him promise that he would not sleep or rest until his message had been transmitted and he was again in Athala with the antidote to the poison that was daily working deeper into Sharka's system. Dagan tried to find some of the scorpions so that if any of the light marks were worn or faded the messenger could renew them for his return, but the only nest he could find had been washed out by the rain and all the scorpions had been drowned. The man said if he found any places that were no longer marked by the scorpion light he would scratch marks with his knife and feel his way along the walls until he found them. He bound his sword to his back so that he would not be hindered by it in the darkness of the conduit and set off.

As each day passed Sharka became progressively ill. On her orders the men dug a deep trench alongside the corral. They threw the remains of Luit's body into it and covered them with a sprinkling of lime they found in a storehouse. They collected the severed and burned heads and what was left of the headless dismembered bodies together and tossed them into the pit as well. Luit's torso sat at the centre of the lifeless debris like a flower overcome by a pestilence.

Sharka watched the macabre process from the comparative dryness of her shelter. She waited for a break in the rain before emerging. She stood at the head of the stinking pit and spoke. Sweat dripped from her feverish forehead but, square shouldered and lithe, with her mop of straw coloured tangled hair falling about her face and onto her shoulders still she looked perfectly elegant and beautiful.

'This is the end of Luit and his flock. It has been my lifetime mission to complete this task. He was my father, and my lover, and I was his murderer. That is the story of it. Do not be distressed by my account.'

It was as though the pronouncement itself was a knife in her bowels. She doubled up with pain, clutching her stomach and vomiting uncontrollably.

Dagan and three others carried her back to the shelter and tried to feed her, but she could not swallow anything and the effort only made her vomit more. Dagan reminded her that he had dispatched the messenger and that he could be expected to return any day soon. Sharka fell asleep and Dagan sat at the entrance to the conduit in the soaking rain, staring into the blackness waiting for the messenger's return. His tears mixed with the downpour and as it washed down his body he felt his remorse soaking into the ground and becoming part of its permanence; that he was responsible for Sharka's situation was more than he could bear and he knew that the fact of it would never change.

It took the messenger three days to work his way through the conduit. He was exhausted when he emerged through the narrow gap beneath the mossy tussock high above the stinking pile of dead bodies built by Graf. He lay at the entrance for a while as his eyes again became accustomed to light. When he could see again, the first thing he saw was Graf working on the wall of corpses, tussling with limbs as he forced them into gaps or repositioned those he felt were in the wrong place. It was tiring work and when Graf rested against a pile of fresh bodies he had brought from the ever filling graveyard outside the walls of Atho, the messenger took his chance and without being seen was soon running down the hillside towards the town.

He found the city gates open and no one in attendance. Still gasping for breath, he went into the church. There he found several dishevelled citizens on their knees mumbling prayers. They did not notice him as he walked

166

down the long aisle that ran between the rows of ornately carved oak pews. He found Treasure sitting behind the altar curtain. She was staring ahead blankly.

'Madam! I am here from Dagan. He says the Mistress Sharka has fulfilled her mission; that Luit is dead, that his followers are destroyed and that your revenge is complete. I am to take the antidote to my mistress as she is already in the later stages of the poison's effects. Time is pressing, madam, and none of it can be wasted. I can only hope the light marks in the conduit will last long enough to allow me to return, for I fear it will take me too long if I have to find my own scratch marks.'

She did not speak.

'Madam! Time is pressing!'

Still she said nothing.

'Madam! I urge you. Come out of your trance. My mistress awaits me. I have promised not to rest until I bring her the cure. Madam, her life hangs on it!'

A bubble of spit expanded from the corner of Treasure's mouth. It filled and burst. Still she did not move.

The messenger grabbed her by the shoulders and shook her. Her jaw dropped and her mouth gaped wide. Her eyes kept staring—unaware of the world her body inhabited, unaware of her being.

'Madam, if this is a meditation, I urge you, wake yourself, please return!'

He dropped to his knees before her. The lines in her face were ingrained with dirt, each one painted a picture of both her age and the time that had passed since she had last cared for herself. It was obvious she had been sitting in this place for many months—this was no trance. She was surrounded by her own urine and defecation. Her arms hung limply by her sides. She was completely unresponsive.

Age and the continuous anxiety of her deep hatred of Luit had slowly taken its toll on Treasure. In the end though, change had come quickly. First she began to lose track of the patterns of her past, then some of the details became transposed in time or confused, then individuals who had populated her mind were forgotten and, in the end, oblique clouds of unknowing covered all that she had been. Faithful to her promise, since Sharka's departure she had kept a servant close by in the church, ready to be dispatched with the remedy to the poison that she had administered. The servant waited until she had no mind left at all and then, after selling the potion she had entrusted to him and stealing her box of jewellery and any money he could find, he went back into the countryside and joined his family a richer man.

Staring into Treasure's vacuous eyes, Dagan's messenger suddenly realised the possibility of not being able to fulfil his mission—he felt empty and lost. An uncontainable anger filled frustration overcame him. He ransacked the little room that Treasure sat in—he turned over tables and chairs, emptied drawers and boxes, tore down the icon of Luit and broke it into pieces—but he found nothing to ease the certainty of failure; there was no antidote and no possessions worth taking. He sat on the floor and listened to Treasure's heavy slow breathing. He knew that somewhere trapped in her vacuous mind was what he needed—the answer, the whereabouts, the explanation. But he also knew that now it was irrecoverable and that his return through the conduit was pointless; if he bore the bad news it would only bring sorrow, and it would be a sorrow compounded by the lack of any alternative. Better, he thought, that others should know nothing of his discovery, better that they believe he had tried his best and had become lost in the dark labyrinth of the conduit. The idea that bad luck had brought about this terrible conclusion would be so much more palatable.

He took the handle of his sword and cracked open Treasure's skull with one heavy blow. He hammered the heavy round pommel into the gap in the fractured bone and knocked her brains out, spilling them all over the shiny stone floor in a lumpy bloody mess. He stared into her shattered face and again demanded a solution to his problem. Her lips

168

trembled and he thought she was going to speak but, instead, a rancid blood striated flow of yellow vomit exploded from her mouth. The hot foul smelling liquor poured over his face and not having time to hold his breath he unavoidably drew it up his nostrils. He jumped up wiping his face frantically and kicked her body angrily. He shouted at her, blaming her for everything that had gone wrong in his life, before walking out into the city filled with hopelessness, remorse and a sense of guilt bred from an unshakeable suspicion that his decision not to return to Dagan and the others was the wrong one.

After a day he passed through a long meadow beneath the blocked entrance to the conduit. Unseen by him, a breathless Lezma peered out of her entrance high above the dead pile. She was resting only long enough to gather enough breath to go back into the labyrinth. Her mind was in turmoil—she could only think of action and that meant movement. She jumped up suddenly and darted through the black tunnels as fast as she could run. She swam in a wild panic to get through the ponds and meres and, as soon as she heard the rain on the Athala side, she turned and started the journey back. Without stopping she ran back to her entrance on the Atho side and, as soon as she saw the light coming from behind the tussock of moss that covered it, she turned and ran again towards Athala.

All the time, in the blackness of the labyrinth, her eyes were wide and panicky, her movements brittle and uncontrolled. As she plunged into the black water of the pools and ponds and swam their width and ran up their opposite shores without stopping, all she could think of was that her master was dead! Her mind could not absorb it. She had told Sharka the story of her exile as if she was recounting a simple instruction given to her by Luit. But it was nothing of the sort. It was only the shock of the knowledge that had caused her to act so impartially, so ridiculously. Even though Luit had banished her from his sight he had always remained her sole hope; she had no other focus. Every day she hoped he would in the end forgive her, she hoped she would dance for him again, and turn cartwheels for him, and run and cling to him when he called. And now it was all over—her hopes were dashed, there was nothing left to hope for and everything had turned to panic. She feared Atho, she had no place in Athala, she could not survive in the conduit, she had nowhere to go. But she had to stop! She did not have the breath to continue!

She burst out of the entrance into the pouring rain of Athala and ran to the pit where the remains of Luit and the flock had been buried. The scattering of lime bubbled on the stinking wet surface of the mud that lay around the strewn bones and flesh.

Lezma broke a branch from a tree, jumped into the pit and used it like a spade to dig amongst the rancid remnants. The pit was filled with deep mud with a shallow skimming of dirty water on its surface. As she dug into it the lime burned her knees, and as the water filled the holes she made with the branch more body parts floated up to its surface.

She tore at the slimy mud with her fingers. She threw sliced off bits of the flock's bodies aside, rolled their burned heads up onto the edge of the pit, and pulled rotting pieces of their viscera from her arms as they stuck to her skin. Suddenly a torso floated to the surface in front of her, it was larger than the rest, cut open and empty. She knew it was Luit—even in this stinking pit she could smell his aroma. She flung herself onto it, embraced it and held onto it desperately.

'Master! Master! Forgive me!' she cried out, her face half buried in the mud and lime. 'Forgive your little imp. I am so sorry. I will never let you down again! Master! Master!'

The already rotting carcass moved beneath her. She grasped her arms around it and kissed every part of it. Her lips burned with the lime and her face was smeared with blood, dirt and entrails.

170

'What must I do? Tell me, master! What must your little elf do?'

Suddenly a head rolled against her face. It was Luit's! She held it and kissed it. She licked her tongue inside the gaping rotten lips. She licked his grey wide eyeballs and clutched the head so close to her face it hurt. But he did not respond and she knew her pleas were empty. Again she was filled with the terror of realising that even if he was prepared to, he was no longer able to redeem her.

She scrambled out of the pit panic stricken. She ran back into the conduit and did not stop until she found herself again at the entrance above the dead pile in Atho. Her heart was pounding and she could not get her breath. The pond below her entrance was now so deep she had to swim all the way across it, and even when she reached the other side she could not find any dry rock to stand on.

Lying in water, she tried to push past the mossy tussock into the open but there was not enough room for her to get out. Black stinking water was streaming past her to the outside but the hole was so small she could not squeeze through. She twisted on her side enough to see that above the entrance a rock fall had blocked the exit. Water spouted out of the small hole left and caused a massive looping black plume that hit the ground a great distance past the base of the dead pile constructed by Graf.

She struggled to breathe and realised that the rancid air was clogging her airways. Her lungs burned and she fought to get air into them. She felt as if she was suffocating. She knew she must find a way out. She dived into the black water and swam down to its bottom. She felt her way along the pile of bodies that blocked the water in a massive rotting dam. Her lungs were bursting and she swam to the surface but there was little relief as again she struggled to breathe the stinking air that rose from the infected black waters of the conduit.

She gasped painfully and, as soon as she could hold enough breath in, she ducked her head beneath the surface and swam down to the bottom. This time she was able to pull a limb free. It was a leg and it floated up beside her as once more she swam frantically to the surface to get at least some air into her scalding lungs. She held her head back on the surface of the water gulping, then again flipped forward, raised her legs clean out of the water and descended into the blackness. This time she managed to pull free an arm and a foot. When she burst to the surface they were already floating there and when she swam back down they churned around her feet as she kicked wildly to get back to the base of the dam.

She found the small hole where she had removed the limbs and squeezed herself into it. She knew as soon as she entered that she would never find her way back. She knew that from here she could only go forward. She did not know how thick the wall of corpses was, and she did not know if she would be able to remove enough to find her way through and, as her lungs burned and became solid with a need for breath, she did no know if she had taken in enough air to complete her task. She began to see lights in her eyes then she felt her mind going blank.

She wriggled forward, all the time her body getting tighter in the narrow hole she had made. She could not move her arms and so bit into the side of a head and with her teeth pulled herself forward against it. She squeezed her shoulders between the compacted thighs and torsos and, her eyes bulging with the strain, she suddenly felt a rushing of water around her cheeks. She wriggled further. The churning water got louder. She could not hold her breath any longer; she felt she had done enough—there was nothing more left. She opened her mouth wide and inhaled—if it was water then she would drown, if it was air she would not; there was nothing she could do to control the outcome.

Her lungs filled with a mixture of water and air. She breathed in again. She vomited and breathed in again. The next moment she found herself ejected from the base of the dead pile in a sudden rush of water that streamed under pressure from the hole she had managed to make.

She lay on her back gasping. She choked and black water burst from her mouth. She inhaled it back up her nostrils. She was dizzy and when she tried to stand up she fell sideways and could not keep upright. Her head reeled. Again she tried to stand. Again she fell over giddily. She was filled with panic. She thought again of running back to Athala, of seeing Luit again, of trying to atone for her misdeeds, of bringing him a gift, and of finding that at last he had forgiven her. She rolled on her side and choked up more black water from her burning lungs. She stared down the unsteady face of the dead pile and saw the hand of a child waving at its base. It seemed to beckon her. Everything went black and as suddenly as it had darkened everything, a dazzling light blinded her.

Still trembling and unsteady she crept down the edge of the pile where Graf had bonded the bodies it constituted into the rocky hillside. Yes, it was the hand of a child and it was being cradled in the arms of its pale and gaunt mother— Medean! Lezma slid on the grassy slope towards them.

She got as close as she dared while at the same time feeling assured she would not be discovered. A grotto had been formed at the base of the dead pile and Medean sat in it cross-legged and preoccupied with her small child. She stroked its lumpy forehead and tenderly pushed back its straggly hair. One of its eyes was grey and unseeing, one of its hands deformed.

Suddenly, the dead pile creaked and Lezma lay flat on the ground in fear. The top edge of the pile swayed as the pressure of water behind strained against it. The plume of black water that looped from Lezma's upper entrance gave a sudden spurt, slowed then shot out with renewed vigour and force. Lezma's eyes followed its path and saw that beyond it the meadows that led down to Atho were already blackened by contamination. The pile stabilised but its top half was now bulging out well beyond the line of the base. Limbs and heads in different stages of decomposition stuck out of it at random angles, some appearing to move as the pressure behind them built then subsided; it was as though the whole wall was waving to her.

Medean sat in the bower that had been shaped into the wall of bodies at the pile's base. Several hands dangled down above her. The child's bed was made from three arms bound together with some entrails. Medean seemed unaware of her surroundings as all the time she petted and fondled the disfigured child. She exposed her breasts and showed it her nipple hoping it would be excited to feed but its crooked split lips could not easily form a seal sufficient to suckle.

The ambling figure of Graf approached pulling a body behind him in each of his massive hands. Medean looked up. For a moment her face was expectant, somehow hopeful, as though seeing him gave her a glimpse of a less nightmarish world, as though she almost thought that the circumstances of her tragic life could change for the better. But as Graf let go of the bodies and stood before her it was obvious from her face that she knew the nightmare would not pass.

'Is my heir well?' he asked in a rough stilted voice.

'He is, my lord. I am about to feed him.'

'That is good for it is time.'

'Time, my lord?'

'Yes, here is the bearer of the news I have been waiting for all my life.'

He reached down and dragged one of the bodies he had brought to its feet. It was the messenger sent by Dagan. He was badly beaten, his jaw was broken and blood streamed from teeth marks in his neck. Graf had found him not far from Atho and when he had attacked him the man had blurted out the story of his mission to find the antidote for the poison now killing Sharka.

'Tell your news!' demanded Graf shaking the messenger. 'Speak!'

The messenger tried to move his broken jaw. Blood and saliva ran over his split bottom lip. He grimaced in pain.

'Speak!' shouted Graf shaking him violently.

The messenger tried again, fighting against the pain and responding to the fear of his ugly and aggressive captor.

'My lady...she is dying...poisoned.'

'By whom?'

'The lady...the lady Treasure.'

'And what of her?'

'She is...she is dead by my own hand.'

'And who is your lady?'

'The mistress Sharka. She has fulfilled her destiny. She has slain Luit and all his followers in Athala and soon she too will die. I have not been able to find the antidote and I fear there is no way back anyway.'

'Are you sure of this? Luit is dead?'

'Yes, it is more than my life is worth to lie, master.'

'Madam! Do you hear that? My half brother is dead. Your daughter is dying. There is no prospect of her survival! And her keeper, Treasure, is dead. At last I can take my empire! At last all obstacles that have stood in my way are gone! At last the kingdom is mine!'

He fell to his knees and held his hands together in prayer.

'Come. We will claim our reward!'

Medean picked up the child and held it to her breasts. She pulled back fearfully from Graf.

'I cannot return. The citizens will reject me. I wish to stay here. This is my sanctuary. I need to feed our child and because of its deformity that is difficult. I cannot lose it.'

'Bring the child!'

'Sir, I cannot. I am too fearful!'

A sudden burst of black water exploded from high up the dead pile. It crossed the spout that flowed from Lezma's entrance, joined it and caused a fractured spiky waterfall that fell in a frantic tumbling cascade to the ground.

Graf rocked from side to side, angered by Medean's resistance. He did not know what to do. He shook the messenger by the neck but the man was completely exhausted by his effort and could not respond—he gaped and stared ahead, no longer concerned about his future life. Graf put the fingers of his right hand behind the man's upper teeth and the fingers of his left hand behind his lower teeth. He held them there for a moment then, still unable to deal with his frustration and with a solution to Medean's resistance evading him, he snapped his hands apart and tore the man's bottom jaw free at the joint. The messenger's lower jaw fell away, held only by the skin of his cheeks and the tension in his throat. His eyes were wide but they could not convey the pain and distress that ran through him. His body went slack. He knew he was not yet dying, he knew there was still more suffering to come, but his resistance had left him just as certainly as life leaves when death intervenes. Graf held him for a few moments then carried him by the neck to the base of the dead pile and stuffed him head first into a fresh hole that was already spewing black water from behind. The man's legs continued to kick as his life entered the final stage of its suffering.

Graf took a rope and tied it tightly around Medean's neck. He pulled her from the safety of the alcove amongst the bodies of the dead pile. She was terrified to be brought out into the open. She held the child tightly to her breasts. It took her nipple and fed clumsily as Graf dragged her roughly away from the leaking dam of bodies and onto the perished meadows that led down to the city walls of Atho.

16. The platinum bell

Graf walked beneath the black water that spewed from the dead pile and mixed with the plume that cascaded from Lezma's entrance above it. Medean and the child were covered in the reeking black pollution. Graf dragged Medean on the rope through the night and late the next day they walked in through the open gates of the abandoned city wall. The few citizens that were in the main square shied away as they approached. Graf lurched at them and spat and they ran into doorways or behind monuments clutching each other in terror.

He yanked at the rope around Medean's neck as she hung back. Tears flowed down her cheeks; they expressed her pain but mostly they told of her humiliation and defilement. The only image she had of her life was her suffering and it was impossible to mask. They entered the church—several praying citizens ran in fear between the pews. They found Treasure's body covered in flies behind the altar curtain. Graf pressed his broken face against the face of the reeking swollen corpse. He stood back and nodded at it, taking the sight as further confirmation of the messenger's story and additional verification of his victory over his half brother Luit and all that he had spawned.

On the hillside above the city, Lezma danced in wild circles. Her fresh face and peach like skin were covered in dirt and blood but her vitality and keenness for life had returned unchanged. The bright city looked like a jewel to her. She performed cartwheels and somersaulted, she fell down and giggled, she ran backwards and hooted and counted up to a hundred then back again to one and all the time jumped and frolicked with irrepressible joy. Gasping for breath, she found a wind bent fir tree and climbed up its sloping trunk. She crouched on the branch and looked down at the city. She started counting the buildings but got confused. She pursed her mud-smeared lips. She thought of Luit, of how he had rejected her and of how much she wanted his forgiveness. She knew that to be pardoned she had to make amends to him—somehow right how she had wronged him. The more she thought about it the more she realised that his exoneration was all she wanted. She bit her lips and plunged her hands between the tops of her naked thighs. She ran her finger along the moist crack of her cunt and resolved to find a way of bringing it about.

She slept on the thick branch with her arms and legs dangling over its sides. When the sun came up she awoke and looked straight down into the city without moving any of her subtle naked limbs. A nest of wild bees at the end of the branch roused themselves for another day—the early workers streaming out in a long curving band into the warmth of the eastern sky. Lezma tightened her thighs against the branch and felt the pressure against the neat slit of her cunt. A ripple of excitement ran through her. She inhaled a waft of her own scent. Her mind filled with her new sense of purpose. She leapt down from the branch and immediately started hooting and cartwheeling down the hillside towards the city walls.

Graf had tied Medean up against the altar of the church for the night. She had fed the baby but most of the time it had failed to satisfy its hunger and cried incessantly. Graf had worked all night in the tower—struggling with something heavy and stumbling and falling as he strained to see in the dim light of the church tower. The next day he found some grain in a store and brought it to Medean—it was impossible for her to eat—dry and filled with husks—and he threw it across the floor angrily. She pleaded with him to release her; she begged to be taken back to the safety of her alcove in the dead pile. It made him even angrier. He shortened the rope between her and the altar so much that she could not pull herself away from it at all. The baby's crying weakened and Medean fought to keep it awake; when she offered it her nipple it did not even try to take it.

Lezma leant against the tree branch. She swatted a bee that buzzed around her face.

'Buzz! Buzz! Buzz!' she shouted at it and giggled. 'I am Lezma the bee hunter! I am hungry and am going to raid your nest like a bear!'

She pranced beneath the nest, jumped up and swiped at it with the flat of her hand. It fell to the ground and split apart. A swarm of irate disturbed bees flew out in a black streaming cloud. Lezma showed no fear of them.

'See, I am a bear. You can buzz all you will, but Lezma the bee hunter is unstoppable!'

She drove her hand into the nest and pulled out a gluey mass of honey. She held it up over her mouth and let it drip between her eager open lips. Bees buzzed round her but her confidence and lack of fear put them on the defensive and they did not dare approach her. They circled her in a cloud but kept themselves at arm's length.

'You are a poor nest of bees! Letting a little bear creep up and steal your crop like this. Look! I do not even have to listen to your buzzing! Lezma the bee hunter can block your chatter out in a second.'

She probed her fingers into the waxy cells made so precisely to contain the fragile young of the swarm and pulled out a mass of wax. She tore and fashioned it into two finger-like pieces. She stuffed one into each of her ears and ran around in a mad dance, screaming and hooting and shouting her defiance to the swarm that still buzzed around her hopelessly. Lezma revelled in her deafness—shouting at the top of her voice, screaming as loudly as she could, yet hearing nothing.

She did not notice the cloudy murk that rose from the blackened meadows as they warmed in the rising sun. She did not notice the black mist rolling down to the city wall, and she did not see it folding in a silent wave over the wall's unguarded top as it entered the city like a massive heavy shroud. She did not hear the screams of the citizens as they ran in panic and she did not hear the sound of a bell echoing through the stinking haze.

The massive platinum bell hung from a heavy rope

Graf had attached to the timber supports high up in the bell tower of the church. Using a mechanism of pulleys and levers, he had spent years hauling it up there. He had attached another rope to its clanger and now at last he stood below it on a specially constructed platform ready to ring it for the first time. He held the hanging rope in both hands placed as high as he could stretch. He inhaled deeply, rose up on his toes and pulled back with all his weight and strength.

He was not prepared for its mesmerising tone—a hollow sound that crushed his eyeballs and pierced his brain. The citizens were woken instantly by its penetrating call. Many rolled from their beds and by the time they fell to their knees were completely mad. Some had time to look in the direction of the sound, and some even to run outside and chase towards its source, but as they emerged into the morning light they were overcome by dizziness and collapsed frothing from their mouths and jerking in painful spasms. Ones that were sleeping in the streets for fear of enclosed spaces managed to run further towards the church but, unable any longer to control their effort, quickly fell breathless to the ground and could not continue. Dogs that sniffed them soon ran in panicky circles, chasing their tails and biting chunks of flesh from their own legs. Some citizens fell under the bell's spell while they still slept. It took form in their dreamy images as a call to another world, or the roar of an animal, or the sound of a sea that had no end. Some saw only an amorphous glitter in their minds. Some saw something solid and watched its gleaming surface as it hovered above them blocking out the sky. Some felt trapped in the shadowy dimness of the night even though they ran into the street and felt the heat of the sun on their skin. Some of these, filled with confusion, huddled together in groups, their eyes filled with bloody tears, blabbering in words not one of them could understand. They thought they gave thanks but they did not know to whom and what their pleas might mean. Some thought they worshipped the ringer of the bell and when they asked others who it was they were told it was a massive vulture that had been conjured up from a handful of emeralds. No one escaped the madness that the bell brought with its ring. Some that were stronger resisted it until the second toll but none more than that. The terrifying magic cast into it by its makers was undiluted and the full power of its corrupting influence flowed out as surely as if it was a stream of pure poison.

Medean's mind went at the first touch of sound—she was directly beneath it and her head was hit by the noise as surely as if she had been struck directly by a bolt of thunder. First she was frozen, then her body went into a seizure against the rope that held her tight against the altar; as the seizure relaxed she was left limp, shaking and drooling. Her face twitched, her eyes strayed in all directions and she saw nothing as she urinated in a continuous and uncontrolled flow. Her head fell to the side as the first ring was completed and she never heard the mighty echo that resounded around the tower in its wake. The child fell from her arms and lay on the floor at her feet; its eardrums had burst and blood ran from its eyes, ears and nostrils.

There was a second ring, and probably a third but Graf was already overcome. The scaffolding he stood on swayed and creaked, the rigging for the bell cracked and split. There was a moment's silence—as if it had all ended and peace had been bestowed—then a huge crash shook the church as the bell fell to the ground on top of Medean.

The edge of the bell cut her in half at the waist before shattering into pieces in a massive explosion that filled the enclosed space with metal fragments. Graf fell after it, still clinging onto the rope he had been using as a pull. He bounced violently from its fractured top, was flung against the wall of the tower and pinioned as a heavy brass candelabrum fixed to the wall penetrated his back and was forced out through his chest. His deformed body dangled on it, twitching down the one side as blood spurted from the wound and ran down the insides of his ill formed legs. He

181

tried for a moment to wriggle free but the madness of the bell had destroyed any sense that was in his hate filled mind. His half blind eyes stared out to an unreachable horizon. On its thin violet edge he saw all that his life could have been: a life of filial love, of bodily perfection and skill, of intellect, and of the admiration of all he met. It was only a glimpse, but in his last moment it showed him a world he had never seen and with it fixed in his shattered mind he died.

Lezma ran through the open gates and into the town square. Her ears were still plugged with the beeswax and she was completely unaware of the sound that had sent every other living thing mad. She chased the string of bees as they flew ahead in a long black thread; the bell had broken their will to look after their hive and they flew only to its call. Lezma jumped up and swatted at them, then cartwheeled or somersaulted before catching them up and swatting at them again. She tried to count them and sent herself into giddy reeling bursts of joy. They led her into the church. She flopped down on a pew and drove her fingers into the slit of her cunt. It was wet and opened at her touch. She had barely drawn her fingers its length when she rose up in a taut seizure of overwhelming ecstasy.

Graf hung pinioned to the wall, the candleholder of the candelabrum that had penetrated him bent and dripping with blood and parts of his lung that had been forced out on its end. He gasped, struggling to breathe as air escaped from the hole the candelabrum had made.

Sweating and panting for breath, Lezma looked around for the bees—they had fled up into the tower and now, having lost any sense of unity, were pouring out as lost individuals and streaming up into the sky only to reach their limit of endurance before dropping back dead. She hooted loudly and spun around in tight circles. She stopped only when she had made herself too dizzy to stand up without falling to the side. She swallowed and realised the wax was still in her ears. She pulled it out and threw it down. Everything was silent except for the sound of Medean's deafened baby struggling to suckle at her mother's breast attached only to the upper part of the body sliced away from the now unseen portion beneath the broken edge of the bell.

Lezma had not entirely escaped the madness of the bell, but the faint sound that had come through to her had merely affected the emphasis she placed on things, on the reality that those things bore, and on how she thought her actions should fit them. Lezma watched the baby cup its hands around Medean's breast and suck—it was all she could see. She listened to it slurping as it fought to nourish itself—that was all she could hear. Her mind was filled with Medean's child; that was all she could think of. She cocked her head to the side. What had Luit said? She tried to remind herself. Take this child? Yes, of course! That was what she must do! She must take it back to him. It was Medean's child, the child he wanted. If she returned it he would forgive her! She scooped it up and it cried loudly as she ran with it back up the hillside to the dead pile.

She found the place at the base of the pile of corpses where she had managed to get through before, but it was impossible to get back into it—the flow of black water was too strong and the wall of bodies compacted too tightly. She ran up to her old entrance, flung the child down and started clearing the rock fall that had blocked it. The cascading plume that issued from the fissure, which had been her entrance and exit, covered her in black stinking water but she did not stop until she had cleared a space large enough to wriggle through.

She dragged the child behind her, unconcerned for its welfare in any way. When she swam through the ponds, she simply pulled it behind her not caring that it was beneath the water's surface and could not breathe. If it struck the rock walls as she twisted and turned through the convoluted labyrinth, she never stopped to check if its injury was harmful or if the child was distressed or suffering.

It was night-time when she emerged into the rain of Athala. She saw that Sharka, Dagan, the men and their

183

servants were all asleep. She crept past them and with the child dangling from her hand she climbed down into the burial pit.

Luit's torso still floated on the surface of the mud surrounded by the dismembered limbs and severed heads of the slaughtered flock. They had continued to rot and the lime had burned irregular holes in any exposed pulpy skin.

Lezma flung herself onto the torso.

'Master! It is I, Lezma! I have brought your child. Look, it is the one you wanted. I have brought it for you and now you will be safe. It cannot harm you now. It can do nothing without your permission. It is like me, sire. Am I not the perfect imp? Let me kiss you. Here, take the child. You can have it within you. Look I will place it where your heart was. What a perfect place. Oh, your imp works so hard for you. Is there anything else, master? Are you satisfied with me at last? Master, have you forgiven me at last? Master, have you forgiven me? Master, please tell me you have forgiven me.'

She pressed the moaning child into his empty carcass, kissed every part of his rotting skin she could reach, asked him again if she was forgiven, turned away and ran from the pit back into the conduit.

Her skin had been burned by the lime in the pit and long scars reached down her arms and legs, her mouth was blistered and reddened and her lips cracked as she opened her mouth wide to gasp in air, but she did not stop. She ran and swam as fast as she could.

When she reached the final pond she tried again to get through the upper exit but the rocks had again fallen and filled it. She dived to the bottom of the stinking water and fought time after time to get through the hole she had used before, but each time she was driven back by a need for air, exhaustion or fear. She managed to release some limbs as before, but still she could not make enough room to squeeze through. In the end, and in complete desperation, she took a massive breath and went down again committed to staying

184

there until she fought her way to freedom or drowned.

As she struggled and laboured, and her lungs burned with the increasing pressure of her used up air, panic spread through her—she felt compelled to get back to Atho and did not know why. A sound formed in her head—a buzzing. Was it the bees? Was it a flock of angry birds? She could not tell. It built to a crescendo then stopped. It was as if she had spiralled headlong through a storm of screaming starlings only to find herself submerged in the swelling sea below. There, drowning, suddenly insulated from their chatter and noise, she stared up open mouthed into the fluttering cloud above the surface of the boiling water. In silence, she watched them as they spun noiselessly in a massive black vortex above the point where she had entered. They were marking her out, pointing to where she was.

All the time, she felt his presence—her master, her beloved Luit. She thought of breathing in—she did not know whether she was or not—but his fragrance filled her full. The touch of that bitter bite at the back of her tongue sent a shiver of joy through her delicate body. Her throat closed. A heave of nausea welled up inside her. She swallowed on it. She wanted to see him again. She was filled with a joyous anticipation. She savoured the taste that foretold the delight of the choking stench of his reeking carcass. She had pleased him at last—she knew it. She had fulfilled her task and he must love her because of it. She quivered with excitement. Bubbles burst in her head. Her heart raced. She licked his odour from her lips. She swilled it down with spit and vomit and she shivered again as his scent exploded from the bubbles of aromatic saliva that entered her stomach. She was suffused with his beastly odour. She was nourished with delight—filled with the ecstasy of him.

A swirl of water burst in a maelstrom around her. A face stared at her. A dismembered leg rubbed against her face. Her lungs filled with the stench of the rancid water and the delightful rotting scent of her master. The next thing she knew she was vomited from the base of the pile as it collapsed. All the carcasses burst out in a great flood and the black water behind them was released in a massive gush. The flood spread down over the meadows towards Atho. It ran across the already blackened fields, through the open gates and into the now still city. It ran up the streets, into the dwellings, storehouses and the church. It lapped at the broken pieces of the platinum bell and took away in its tide the severed torso of Medean and the fallen icon of Luit that Sharka had slept beneath for all her growing years.

17. Dagan's sorrow

Near the entrance to the conduit in Athala they heard the rush of water from the labyrinth as the dam of the dead gave way. No one knew what it was, but no one spoke for a while after it had passed.

Dagan stayed close to Sharka day and night. She drifted in and out of consciousness. Sometimes she spoke lucidly; sometimes she spoke in what seemed an ancient tongue and Dagan could not understand her. He became increasingly desperate to receive news from the messenger. He chose a second man to go and look for him. The man was nervous to set out alone but did so anyway. Listening at the entrance Dagan soon heard the man's desperate cries as he called for help, having lost his way within a few hours. Dagan sent another two, but they met the same end. Dagan said that any of the men or servants who wanted to try and return to Atho was free to do so. They searched for scorpions' nests so that they could mark their journey but every one of them had been washed out and no scorpions were found alive. All of the men and servants decided to try the journey nevertheless. Dagan helped equip them with tapers and torches and in a long line they set out into the labyrinth. The lights flickered and went out as soon as they entered, but they carried on. Dagan listened at the entrance until their footsteps could no longer be heard. A little later he heard someone cry out in pain as though injured but after that there was nothing.

Dagan felt happier alone with Sharka, it was more private and he could give her all his attention. The nights had become cold and the incessant rain chilled them continuously. One night the rain turned to sleet and Sharka shivered uncontrollably. While she was asleep Dagan brought her black fur cape and wrapped it around her as well as he could. She awoke a little later and with great effort she managed to pull it up around her shoulders. She sat up and closed it against her chest with squarely folded arms. Dagan thought she looked exactly the same as when they had found the men in Oskia.

Suddenly, the icy rain stopped. The air was filled with the sound of drips against the background of the surprising silence. The stillness reinvigorated her and for a while she paced about staring vacantly ahead as though in a trance. She strode in an uninterrupted diagonal line in and out of the shelter then returned and re-crossed her former path as if describing an unseen cross. But the monotonous, rhythmic movement of her pacing unsettled her and, in the end, unable to bear it any more, she told Dagan it was time to sleep.

'I will sleep with the men as usual. I love to step between them, to hear the sounds of their breathing and the shuffling of their uncomfortable bodies. Dagan, all of it relaxes me. Sometimes I wonder what dreams they have that make their limbs twitch. Look, Dagan look at this one, he must be having a dream filled with delights!'

Dagan nodded, his eyes filled with tears.

'Dagan, I see on their sleeping faces the emptiness of their bodies. You know their spirits fly away when they dream. That is where they are now, flying. I will lie between them and feel their heat. I will be uncomfortable with them, share their mortal discomfort, and when I twitch, if you watch me, you will know I am flying with them, that my spirit has left my body for a few hours of freedom. Yes, Dagan, watch me fly with them.'

The rain held off and Sharka spent the night sitting at the dark gaping mouth of the conduit. She had lost sight of the men—the image of them had passed with the closing darkness of the night. She felt expectant, as though someone would come and save her, but, as the sun showed itself in thin red ribbons across a rarely seen clear sky, she knew she had been abandoned. The dull light again found its accustomed greyness and picked out the pallor of her high cheekbones. She did not turn to look into the conduit but she could sense her shadow being cast on its back wall deep

188

inside. She imagined herself the reality of that murky image but knew that in truth she was only the puppet of a master whose motive was beyond her understanding. She imagined how she dangled on the strings hanging from his fingers— falling this way and that, drooping her head and suddenly looking up in surprise when he twitched the strand that ran into the top of her head. A sense of warmth ran through her. She sensed a life beyond her mortality—stretching back to a time before it had begun and forward beyond when it would end. Had she sat here before she wondered? Would there be a time in the future when she would return? Only he knew— the eternal one, the puppet master, the knower who controlled her. If it were to be so then his messenger would arrive with news of her salvation. But she had waited all night, shivering in the darkness, feeling a new sense of weakness, alert for the sound of his approaching steps—and she had heard nothing. Yes, he must have abandoned her. Thrown her strings to the ground and moved on. He had dispatched no messenger and now he would dismiss her from the world.

Dagan came and sat at her feet. He looked deeply into her eyes. He sensed she was abandoning him and, for the first time since he had known her, she smiled at him. Her bright teeth glistened in the weak sun and she stretched out her hand and brushed her fingers tenderly across his forehead.

'Dagan. You know what will happen?'

He could not reply. The tears that were welling up inside him made it impossible.

'You will have to tend me. Make sure I am safe.'

He nodded as the tears flowed down his cheeks.

'I have a little time, a day or two, maybe even a third. Tonight you can tell me everything you wish. You can keep me warm.'

She clasped her arms around her chest and shivered. She reached out and stroked Dagan's tears. He noticed her hand was shaking.

'If we find that servant who stole the horse, and I am too ill to recognize him or take my revenge, I leave him to you. Post men each hour to stay awake and wait for a message. It may yet still come. If the messenger comes he will be weary and slow, the guards must run on ahead of him and tell me so that I know not to die before he arrives. Dagan, you have served me well. Since we first met you have cared for me. Do you remember? When I was only a child? From now on, take orders only from yourself. In following your own course you will be responding to my every wish. Do not speak to me again. I could not bear it.'

The day passed and another night came. Sharka again waited at the mouth of the conduit but did not speak. The messengers did not come.

Another day passed. Dagan huddled near a smoky fire he had lit; he was trying to learn how to face his future loneliness, but the anticipation of it only produced anxiety and fear.

Sharka moved further into the conduit. She sensed her removal from the world of shadows. Even with her eyes closed, she saw the glimmer of reality beyond the dim captive shadows in the cave.

She became feverish again and vomited; the poison was running deeply in her veins, the gloss of life that had flashed across her skin for the last few days was turning into an ashen haze.

As she stared out from the misty entrance to the abysmal labyrinth of the conduit, she finally exhaled her last mortal breath. It was a bitter breath, short and gasping, as though she was choking on her last fleeting experience of life. Her eyes were still open as the glitter gradually faded from them. Their diminishing brightness was etched with a greying opalescence—a creeping cataract of death. The shimmering strands of the boiling sun that had flecked her healthy cheeks in Atho were no longer there. They had remained on the sea beyond the dunes, as remote as the bright shafts that had exploded from behind the jutting peaks that could only be seen from the city's towers all those years ago. She had left them to their own course, and she would die now, abandoning them to their own dark future.

Dagan held her in his arms for several hours, looking down at her white face and occasionally bending to kiss her cold, blue lips. She looked so beautiful—a creation of the gods. Each time he kissed her pallid lips he hoped it would awaken her—that she would shudder, then breathe, then gasp and shout out in shock at having been drawn back from what would be a half-remembered death. But no, even though he licked his warm tongue against her cooling flesh, and wished that some of his life would pass to her, nothing happened; there was no magic, no miracle. He thrust his tongue deeply into her mouth, as though he could excite her back from the dead, but he felt only the icy coldness of death over her drying lips. He felt ashamed of his actions and his eyes reflected his sense of embarrassment. He felt humiliated by his violating act. He wanted to withdraw it—as if it was something he could rub out or correct—but he felt the darkness of its immutability as it took its place with her in the unending world of unchanging fact.

Finally, he laid her down on the muddy ground and rolled her on her side. He wished for a gold-encrusted barge to furrow the beach with its pointed bow and for her servants—wearing festive robes and decked with green garlands—to lift her up reverently and carry her to the waiting vessel. He wanted to see her tangled blonde hair snagging on the wooden sides of the ship as strong brown arms passed her out of the light and into the dark of the vessel's creaking hold. He imagined her servants standing by his side as the boat was pushed out into the waves, steered only by her most faithful acolyte who would himself now perish willingly in the flames that would consume her ice-cold body. One of the servants would pass Dagan the flaming torch. He would take it slowly—no longer compelled to act with urgency, or with concern for the future. His face would show his uncertainty and his tearful

191

eyes would testify to his grief, but he would not be able to refuse his role. He would feel the sizzling black pitch dripping onto his arm and would be aware of his apathy at its searing bite as it burned his flesh. He would sense the strange quietness that preceded the last act, and a feeling of finality would wind around him like a shroud. He would throw the burning torch and watch it curve through the air before plunging down into the darkness of the burial chamber within. The fated coxswain would glance back to the shore, as if to take one final glimpse of life, and then the boat would explode in flames, consuming Sharka and sending her remains into the sky on curling plumes of hot and reddened air.

Dagan looked down at Sharka and the reality of it all. He wanted to cry, but there was nothing left in him—he felt dried-out and empty. Behind his misty wet eyes he imagined one of her men running frantically towards him, shouting out the news in gasping breaths, shouting excitedly that the one who his mistress had been expecting had come at last and would be here within the hour.

He bent his face to her one last time—another kiss, another second of closeness. He closed his eyes and waited for the moment of departure, knowing he would never take the risk of this terrible intimacy again. He felt a drop of rain against his cheek. He thought he must quickly get her back under shelter, then he realised that it would be pointless. Another drop, then another, and he turned his face to the side—in part to shelter her from the rain—just as she lifted her head, opened her mouth and sank her teeth deeply into his exposed neck. The shadowy image that was Sharka in the real world—her appearance in the world of only appearance—now reflected a new form; one that blended her previous irreality with the reborn shape and form of her father Luit.

As Dagan screamed and she reared up and dug her teeth in deeper, a fleeting form darted between the soaking trees.

Lezma's eyes lit up as they followed the scream to its source. She was saved!

'Master! You are back! You have forgiven me!'

Epilogue

Today they will be exalted, but tomorrow they will not be found, because they will have returned to the dust, and their plans will have perished.

1 Maccabees 2. 63

And so all that was before arrives in the present, and all that will come after is only a present hope. Everything changes; nothing is immune from alteration. Nothing occurs now without notice although we do not know the events that paint its pattern. Fate is the only certainty and that is unknown until it occurs. Everything affects everything that follows it, and everything is an effect of all things that have gone before it. Nothing is outside the cycle of change and influence, though there are many cycles within cycles. One of these cycles is a life.

And so another cycle is complete; another turn of the world is made entire.

All of us die, and from our disappearance the future world is shaped. The presence of our lives is preceded by a history that brings us into now, and this moment of existence—this present spot in time—is shaped by all that has caused it to be. A time is only ever before or after us—a time is only ever good or bad and that judgment is only in the minds of those that live it.

47016603R00114

Printed in Poland
by Amazon Fulfillment
Poland Sp. z o.o., Wrocław